YOU LIGHT UP MY MIDLIFE CRISIS
GOOD TO THE LAST DEATH, BOOK FIVE

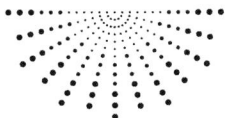

ROBYN PETERMAN

Copyright © 2021 by Robyn Peterman

All rights reserved.

No part of this book may be reproduced in any form or by any electronic or mechanical means, including information storage and retrieval systems, without written permission from the author, except for the use of brief quotations in a book review.

This book is a work of fiction. Names, characters, places, and incidents either are the product of the author's imagination or are used fictitiously. Any resemblance to actual persons, living or dead, businesses, companies, events, or locales is coincidental.

This book contains content that may not be suitable for young readers 17 and under.

Cover design by *Cookies Inc.*

Edited by *Kelli Collins*

PRAISE FOR THE GOOD TO THE LAST
DEATH SERIES

"Daisy's life has been turned upside down, and we get to watch the aftermath. Prepare to root for a new heroine. You'll fall in love with this hilarious hoyden and all of the hot water she dives into. Head first! Masterful and heartwarming, don't let this one get away!"
—NY Times Bestselling Author Darynda Jones

"Brilliant and so relatable! I laughed, I cried, I swooned, and I sighed. Heavily. Robyn Peterman has her finger on the pulse of midlife madness, and I can't get enough."
— USA Today Bestselling Author, Renee George

"I'd read the phone book if Robyn Peterman wrote it! It's A Wonderful Midlife Crisis is a home run of hilarious, heartwarming paranormal fun. Midlife's a journey. Enjoy the ride. Crisis included… Read it!"
— Mandy M. Roth, NY Times & USA TODAY Bestselling Author

"Hilarious, heartbreaking, magical and addictive! No one can turn a midlife crisis upside down quite like Robyn Peterman. A stay-up-all-night novel that will have you begging for more."

— *Michelle M. Pillow, New York Times and USA Today Bestselling Author*

ACKNOWLEDGMENTS

This series has been in my head for two years. It took a call and a nudge from Shannon Mayer to make me pull the file out and finish book one. Now you're getting book five! Each word was a joy to write and I owe Shannon for yanking me into the Paranormal Women's Fiction group. Playing in a sandbox with strong talented women who have each other's backs is a rare and special experience.

As always, while writing is a solitary experience getting a book into the world is a group project.

The PWF 13 Gals — Thank you for a wild ride. You rock.

Renee — Thank you for all your support, your friendship, your formatting expertise and for being the best Cookie ever. You saved my butt on this one. Forever in your debt. TMB. I promise I will get our phrase into the next book. LOL

Wanda — Thank you for knowing what I mean even

when I don't. LOL You are the best and this writing business wouldn't be any fun without you.

Kelli — Thank you for saving me from scary grammar mistakes. You rock. And thank you for letting me be late… again. LOL

Nancy, Susan, Heather and Wanda — Thank you for being kickass betas. You are all wonderful.

Mom — Thank you for listening to me hash out the plot and for giving me brilliant ideas. You really need to write a book!

Steve, Henry and Audrey — Thank you. The three of you are my world. Without you, none of this would make sense. I love you.

DEDICATION

This one is for Henry and Audrey. You inspire me everyday.

MORE IN THE GOOD TO THE LAST DEATH SERIES

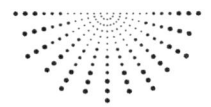

PREORDER BOOK SIX NOW!

BOOK DESCRIPTION

YOU LIGHT UP MY MIDLIFE CRISIS

Midlife is definitely a journey. The road has massive potholes.
And the crisis... it's the gift that keeps on giving.

Being forty is supposed to be freaking fabulous not fatal.

Taking on a daunting new job minus the description isn't the smartest move I've ever made, even if it was to save a friend. Hopefully, it doesn't turn out to be the stupidest... or deadliest.

Why can't things stay the way they were? I love my old job. Supergluing ghosts back together and solving their issues is its own reward. Not to mention, I'm seriously good at it. Although, I must say, I'm ridiculously excited for the new Death Counselor's arrival in nine months...

BOOK DESCRIPTION

Adding to my problems, there are four new angels in town who are riding my butt and judging every move I make. Literally. Who knew destroying one Immortal could cause me so much trouble? If I'm found guilty, I'll be pushing up daisies.

Luckily, my nutty friends have my back and the Grim Reaper has my heart. What could possibly go wrong?

Nothing is impossible. I am living proof. Let's just hope I live to prove it.

CHAPTER ONE

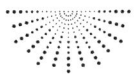

"Holy shit," Jennifer shouted, skidding to a stop with Charlie right behind her. "Is that a floating arm?"

While I was used to random arms and legs lying around, Jennifer was not. "It is," I said, pulling her back and shooting Tim a look.

I didn't know what was happening. But I did know that Jennifer was one hundred percent human. There was no way I wanted her near a floating arm. I had no idea if anything else was attached to it.

"On it," Tim said, leading Jennifer a safer distance away.

"The hand is holding June's soul," Charlie cried out. "We still have fifteen minutes to get it back in her."

His hope for his beloved wife was contagious, and a collective sigh of relief was exchanged amongst everyone. As Charlie slowly walked toward the hand, the soul orb twinkled briefly then disappeared.

His knees buckled and he went down like a broken man.

The Immortal Enforcer was one of the most powerful people I knew. Right now, Charlie was a mere shell of himself.

"No," I hissed. "Unacceptable." I had a sick feeling I knew who the hand belonged to. I'd immediately narrowed it down to four people—for lack of a better word. "Show yourselves, you lying cowards."

Again, without fanfare.

Again, without wind or lightning.

The Angels arrived.

The four stood in a row in my decimated front yard where a celestial war had just taken place—a war they were supposed to have refereed. Rafe, Gabe, Abby and Prue might look angelic, but to me they were trash. Weak, lying, horrible people. The blood on their hands from today could have been massive. They hadn't shown up until the death and destruction was over. From the bored expressions on their faces, it was clear they didn't care. Their pretty exteriors belied putrid insides.

June's soul was perched in Prue's hand.

"You're late," I snapped.

"You're rude," Prue countered.

"Well, no thanks to you, I'm still here," I said. "You have something that belongs to me." I held my hand out for the soul.

"And you have information that belongs to us," Abby reminded me with a sour expression on her otherwise beautiful face.

"Terms were broken," I said in an icy tone. "You didn't

hold up your end. You snooze, you lose. Give me the soul. I'm the Death Counselor. It belongs to me."

"Interesting you should mention that," Rafe commented, staring at Clarence while speaking to me. He nudged Gabe and nodded in my father's direction.

Gabe stared with rapt fascination.

Was the Archangel Michael a rock star in Heaven? From their reactions, I'd have to go with a yes. Otherwise, it was just weird.

"Stop staring at him," Abby hissed. "He's nothing."

Abby was a bitch. I was kind of done with bitches for the foreseeable future. However, they had something I wanted.

"The Archangel Michael is *not* nothing," Heather said, stepping up to my side. "He's a more honorable Angel than any of you could ever dream of becoming."

Rafe raised a brow and Gabe chuckled. "Not surprising," Gabe said, referring to Heather's words. "However, I wonder if she would jump to his defense if she knew."

"Knew what?" my father inquired, eyeing the quartet warily.

Abby's expression grew uglier. "That she's your *daughter*," she hissed.

"She already knows," my father said in a frigid tone that gave the four Angels pause. "That is none of your business. I'd suggest we move on."

The four were silent as they exchanged glances. Rafe shrugged and turned his attention back to me. "As I was saying, it's interesting that someone who killed an Angel would think she still had the job of Death Counselor."

Were they serious? Clarissa had a bounty on her head

that was their damned responsibility to take care of. The assholes had left their dirty work to me and were now trying to punish me for doing their job. Not to mention, Clarissa had tried to kill my father and me. It had boiled down to her or us. The choice had been a no-brainer.

"Enough," Gideon growled. "Just because you were too fucking fragile to do your damned duty when you knew the crimes committed and the punishments that were to be doled out, you will not pass judgment on the one who did your foresworn work. Am I clear?"

Prue laughed and eyed Gideon with female appreciation. I wanted to slap her.

"You have no jurisdiction in our community," she said with a dismissive wave of her hand. "Fallen Angels are beneath us."

"Far beneath," Gabe added with a condescending smile at Gideon.

"It would give me great pleasure to behead all of them," Gideon said.

"That might be a little much," I told him. *"We still have to get June's soul and put it back in her."*

"Fine," Gideon agreed begrudgingly. *"However, I'm leaving the option open."*

"You dicks are correct for once. The Grim Reaper does not have jurisdiction," Candy Vargo announced, coming out from behind my father. I almost laughed. She had waited to make an entrance. It was fabulous. "But, as the Keeper of Fate, I have jurisfuckingdiction everywhere, assholes. Nice to see you losers again. Did ya miss me?"

The Angels backed away quickly. While it was every

kind of awesome to see the Angels' fear, it might not be helpful.

"Thank you, Candy Vargo," I said. "I'd say the Angels are appallingly thrilled to see you. If I need your assistance, I will *definitely* ask for it. You feel me?"

I still had no clue what Candy Vargo had done to the Angels, but it was obviously heinous.

"Okey-dokey," Candy said, blowing a kiss to the Angels and stepping back.

"You know what?" I glared at all four. "I'm really tired. Today has sucked so far. Get to your bottom line. I need to eat and then sleep. But right now, I have about fourteen minutes to get that soul back to its rightful owner. It might be a serious blemish on your records if you kill an innocent."

"Not to mention, she's the human wife of the Immortal Enforcer," my father added in a tone that made them think twice.

Charlie was literally shooting silver flames from his eyes. I could tell he was gauging what would happen if he simply went for June's soul.

I didn't want to find out.

"If I tell you what's in the book, will you give me the soul?" I asked quickly before Charlie took the matter into his own dangerously sparking hands.

Prue smiled. It didn't reach her eyes. Part of me thought I was insane to trust them again since they'd lied already. But the clock was ticking. If there was a chance to get June's soul without anyone else being incinerated today, that was the way to go.

"Yes," she said.

"Immediately?" I asked.

She rolled her eyes. "Yes."

"Unharmed. In one piece?" I pressed. I wasn't leaving anything to chance this time. The Angels were a very literal bunch.

"Yessssss," she hissed.

Heather pointed at her watch, then tossed me the notebook with the translation from the book. There was no time to waste. I knew it might backfire, but we were at the point of no return for June. My gut told me to take the risk.

Clearing my throat, I read, "Out with the old. In with the new. Strange happenings are on the horizon. Paths will converge and truths shall be revealed. The future lies in the deadly hands of one. Choices will be made. Who makes the choices and what choices are made remain to be seen."

All four of the Angels laughed.

"As I predicted," Rafe said. "But before we return the soul, I'd just like to point out that none of you here have the ability to put it back in without killing your friend."

That was not what I wanted to hear.

"Can you?" I demanded, wondering what price I would have to pay to make that happen. Whatever it was, I would gladly pay it.

"Interestingly, no," Rafe said. "It was removed by the Angel of Mercy. It must be replaced by the Angel of Mercy."

"That might present a little problem," I snapped. "Did you know this all along? You got what you wanted, knowing I wouldn't get what I wanted?"

"All you asked for was the soul," Abby reminded me with

a brittle smile. "You didn't say anything about the safe return to the owner."

"Are all of you flying freaks so damn literal?" Candy demanded.

"We are," Gabe said, backing away a little.

"Disgusting," my father said, staring daggers at the group. "A deplorable representation of our kind."

"Be that as it may," Rafe said, uninterested in rising to the bait. "As the text said, there are choices to be made. Who makes the choices and what choices are made remain to be seen."

I blew out an exasperated breath and willed myself not to imprison them in an iron cage. "Riddles won't work. I have ten minutes."

"The Angel of Mercy job is open, *Daisy*," Prue said. "You might want to think about taking it."

"Are you out of your freaking mind?" I shouted. "I'm the Death Counselor. There are no others. I'm the last one. The balance would be thrown off and that would cause a shit-show. And that's only one of the problems. I'm not Immortal—which I would think is a huge issue. Plus, there is no way in hell I would be able to send souls to the darkness. That's not how I roll. But hey, here's an idea to chew on. Why don't one of you take over the job to make up for fucking up today?"

"Daisy," Gram snapped. "While shit and damn are just fine in a pinch, we do not drop the f-bomb."

I closed my eyes and nodded contritely. "Sorry, Gram."

"I say fuck all the time," Candy Vargo pointed out.

"Yep, I know," Gram said. "We're gonna tackle that after we get you to shave your legs regularly."

"Fuck," Candy muttered.

My father seemed as confused as I was. As were Gideon, Heather and Tim. Charlie was still plotting how to get June's soul back while causing as much harm to the Angels as possible.

And we had less than ten minutes.

"I can't be the Angel of Mercy," I said, trying to make them understand. "For all the reasons I told you. I'm the Death Counselor. I'm good at it and I love it."

"You are not the only Death Counselor," Gabe said. "Your arrogance is astonishing."

"Actually, yours is," I muttered. "Where is this other Death Counselor?"

"She will arrive soon," Rafe said.

"Okay," I said, ready to headbutt him. "I'll bite. Define soon."

The Angel's eyes traveled down my body. It didn't feel sexual to me, more curious. However, Gideon growled and put his arm around me possessively.

"Answer me," I insisted. The Angel was cruising for a deadly bruising from the Grim Reaper.

"Nine months," he replied, staring at my stomach.

I grabbed Gideon so I didn't hit the dirt. My knees felt shaky and I was positive I'd misinterpreted.

Candy cackled. "We're gonna have a baby to spoil," she shouted.

Maybe I hadn't.

My gaze jerked to her. "We use condoms," I shouted.

"Don't matter," she said, still grinning like a fool. "What's fated is fated. I just didn't think Gideon's little swimmers would work anymore. He's old."

Gideon's arms tightened around me.

"I don't..." he began.

"Know what to say?" I finished for him.

"I'm shocked," he said.

I was thrilled. I couldn't help it. I wanted to scream and dance with joy. But there were two issues standing in my way. The Angels didn't deserve to see my happiness. Most importantly, I had no clue how Gideon felt.

"Happy shocked. Or horrified shocked?" I asked, then held my breath.

"Overcome with joy shock. Over the moon shocked. Humbled shocked, but..."

"But?" I asked.

"But it's your decision," he said, tempering his elation.

There was no time to play games. I wasn't a game player anyway. *"I love you. I want the baby we made together. You have made me the happiest woman in the world. We good?"*

"More than good," Gideon replied. *"We're also running out of time."*

He was right. Charlie was ready to explode.

My earlier thoughts raced through my mind and consumed me with guilt. Why was there even a doubt in my mind? I had the chance to save one of my dearest friends. Only minutes ago, I wondered the price I would have to pay to make June whole again. I was certain whatever it was I would gladly pay it... yet, now I wasn't as sure.

My mind was a chaotic hot mess. I went back to my old standby... a list.

Was this going to make me Immortal? Probably a good question to ask.

Could I stand living forever? I couldn't answer that. I was forty.

Would it be an issue if I wasn't sure I believed in God? Most likely.

Could I make the decision to send ghosts to the darkness? Probably not.

I would be in direct opposition with the man I loved and the soon-to-be father of our child. Would that cause a wall between us? Again, no clue.

Could I live with myself if I didn't save June's life?

No. I could not.

I had the muddiest clear answer in the world. And I was going with it.

"Five minutes," Charlie said tersely.

"Yes," I said, taking June's soul from Prue's hands. "The answer is yes. I will be the Angel of Mercy."

"Excellent," Prue said. "And so, it shall be recorded," She waved her hand and shimmering yellow crystals fell from the sky and covered the lawn. "Daisy Leigh Amara-Jones shall henceforth be graced with the title the Angel of Mercy."

"That's it?" I asked.

"That's it," Prue confirmed. "Job is yours now whether you change your mind or not. You're stuck."

I nodded. "I have to go," I said, turning and moving toward the house.

"Wait," Abby snarled. "Is that a human?" She pointed at Jennifer in shocked surprise.

"I am," Jennifer said.

"And you were witness to all of this?" Abby demanded.

"Damn straight," Jennifer confirmed with a thumbs up. "Much better than *Twilight*."

"Unacceptable," Abby hissed, waving her hand in a circular motion at Jennifer.

Jennifer cried out and fell to the ground.

"What did you do to her?" Tim roared, sounding scarier than I'd ever heard him. "ANSWER ME."

"She'll be fine, Courier," the bitchy Angel growled. "I wiped her memory of all of this. She has not been harmed."

"Says you," Tim snapped, picking up Jennifer carefully and shielding her from further abuse.

"Oh," Rafe yelled as I took the porch steps two at a time. "A couple more things."

I paused with my back to him. I seriously didn't have time for this. "What?" I turned and faced the arrogant ass.

"Be prepared to fail. Reintroducing a soul into a human body is rarely successful."

"Fuck you," Candy snarled at him. "Might have wanted to start with that upfront."

He shrugged and laughed. "Daisy will still be brought up on charges for killing her predecessor. A tribunal shall be announced shortly."

"Is that all?" my father demanded, walking menacingly toward the Angels.

"Almost... *Dad*," Rafe said. "I'd say it was nice to finally meet you, but it's not."

The Archangel stopped dead in his tracks. My father stared at the Angels. There was little to no emotion coming from either side.

"Wait. What?" Heather shouted. "We're related to those lying shitbags?"

And the world kept spinning off its axis. I'd have to absorb the stomach-churning news of my extended family later. There were far more important matters at hand than being distantly related to assholes.

"Go, go, go!" Charlie shouted. "Three minutes."

Using my freakish speed, I raced up the stairs. My friends were right behind me.

This had to work.

Screw the Angels. They'd lied about other things. They could have lied about this.

"Stay with me, June," I whispered as I touched her icy coffin. "I need you back. Charlie needs you to come back. We all need you."

Winning was the only option.

I was the new Angel of Mercy.

I was making new rules—and losing was out of the question.

CHAPTER TWO

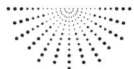

THE LIFE-AFFIRMING AFTERNOON SUNLIGHT STREAMING through the windowpane was in stark juxtaposition to the scene in front of me. With only a little over two minutes to go, I stared at my dear friend. Feeling light-headed and ready to hurl, I wondered if becoming the Angel of Mercy came with extra knowledge. It certainly didn't seem like it. I had no damn clue what to do.

"Everyone, back away," Gideon said, slashing his hand through the air over June's frozen tomb.

Sparks of blood-red fire left his fingertips engulfing the bedroom in an eerie glow. For the briefest of moments, I was alarmed that none of what was happening felt strange or foreign to me. The unbelievable and impossible had become my normal.

Several of my deceased roomies huddled in the corner of the bedroom to watch—including the gal I called the

Tasmanian Devil. She was a wild one with a penchant for scaring people by hiding in drawers and popping out unexpectedly, but she appeared curious and calm. I wasn't sure it was a good idea to have them here, but there was no time to shoo them away. I was down to nine dead guests. Not too long ago there had been over fifty, give or take a few. Since they could float right through each other it was difficult to count them.

Gideon waved his hand again. The ice that had encased June melted away. There was no puddle of water—no evidence that she'd been interred in a frozen coffin. June's body wasn't blue or swollen. She simply looked like she was sleeping on the bed in my sunny guestroom. She wasn't. Technically she was dead… or almost dead. And it was my job to save her.

There were a few problems.

The tension was high and the silence was deafening. My father stood at the foot of the bed. My mom and Gram floated in the air next to him. Missy and Heather held hands and stood in the open doorway. Tim and Candy Vargo flanked Gideon. The three stood right behind me. Charlie placed himself at my side and didn't take his eyes off of his wife.

My heart raced as fast as my mind. Scanning the room, I hoped to the darkness and back that someone at some time in their absurdly long life had witnessed what I was about to try… or at least something similar. I wasn't sure what *similar* would entail, but I was willing to take any advice I could get.

"Quick question," I said, hoping I didn't sound as freaked out as I felt. "On the outside chance that anyone has seen this before, I could use a hand."

No one said a word.

"Anyone?" I asked.

Silence.

"Any ideas?" I asked, staring helplessly at the shimmering golden orb in my hand.

"We could open her mouth and shove it in," Candy Vargo suggested, sounding as unsure of herself as I'd ever heard her.

"Mmkay," I said, staying neutral. Candy could be violent. "That doesn't feel right, but thank you."

"What about handing it to her?" Tim tried.

"She's kind of half-dead right now," I pointed out. "Not sure that would work."

Tim nodded. He still held a passed-out Jennifer in his arms. "I see your point. I'm going to take Jennifer elsewhere. If she wakes up, she won't understand since the deplorable Angels took her memory of who we truly are."

"Yes," my father said. "Do that."

Tim left without a sound.

I dove into the minds of the dead. I transported Missy when she was in danger. I ran at the speed of light. I knocked down trees with my hands. I could do this. I had to do this.

"I'm going with my gut," I whispered. There was too much to lose. Grasping at straws right now was all I had. I sent up a quick, silent prayer to God. I still wasn't positive I believed, but by taking on the job of the Angel of Mercy it was a fairly safe assumption he or she was my boss.

"Ask more questions, Daisy," Gideon said, placing his hand on my shoulder. "Talk it out."

I nodded jerkily. Gideon's touch centered me. Time was ticking. Charlie was like a bomb about to explode. Considering Charlie was the Immortal Enforcer, that could be very bad indeed. "Where does a soul live in the human body?"

"The soul lives in the heart of a human," my father said. "The heart is the first organ to appear during embryonic development. The soul guides the heart and the heart protects the soul."

Awful visions of Candy Vargo carving Gideon's chest with a dagger for the black magic ritual were stuck in my head. That was a no-go. June was human. She wouldn't survive being carved like a turkey so I could place her soul directly on her heart.

"The heart encompasses love," my mother whispered.

Charlie reached out and touched the deathly still June. "Love is the hushed feeling that's the catalyst for the next breath of air you take. The entirety of love means that when it's gone, broken pieces become obvious to the naked eye. What is strong becomes weak. It's intangible—no spoken word can truly make sense of it. I know this to be true. My search spanned millions of years. I never found love until June. She's my oxygen and my reason." He paused, then turned his bright silver gaze on me. "Just try, Daisy. If June's demise is fated, it will be as it should be."

Charlie was correct. The only way to truly fail was not to try.

My breath caught in my throat. The responsibility was overwhelming. My love for June was different than Charlie's, but it was strong and real. And I understood what he meant. I felt the same for Gideon.

Nodding again, I let my heart take over. "Take my hand, Charlie. Gideon, touch my back," I instructed. The soul orb in my hand twinkled. I took it as a good sign. "Charlie, imagine June alive and whole. Picture her in your mind."

"As you wish," he whispered, closing his eyes and gripping my hand in a tight embrace.

My next question felt strange and wondrous at the same time. "Gideon, can you protect our child?"

I felt his smile even though he stood behind me. "I can and I will."

My relief was extreme. I'd never been someone's mother, yet the fierce need to protect the tiny person inside me was all-consuming.

As the Grim Reaper, Gideon represented darkness. I was banking on me embodying light. The intertwining of the light and dark was needed for balance. Charlie symbolized love and justice. The power of three. An atrocity had been done to June by Clarissa. I had a chance to right the wrong.

"Candy Vargo, sing," I directed.

"Sing what?" she asked.

"I don't know," I said as a bizarre sense of calm washed over me. "Just pick something pretty and make sure it's in a dead language."

"Can do," she said with a grin.

The melody was haunting. It filled the room and bounced lightly off the walls in a surreal and enchanted way. A buzz vibrated under my skin. Leaning down, I kissed June's soft cheek and gently placed the glimmering golden soul orb on her chest over her silent heart. I felt both Charlie's and Gideon's power and strength in their touch. Without thinking, I took my free hand and cupped June's cheek. The connection was shocking and searingly painful. Sucking my bottom lip into my mouth so I didn't cry out, I hoped that June wasn't experiencing the same pain. Hopefully, if she was, she wouldn't remember.

Gideon's hand tightened on my shoulder as the sensation of blazing-hot knives ripped through my body and tore me apart. Standing rigidly still and keeping my connection to June, I gritted my teeth and bore it. I was sure my skin had melted from my bones, but no one shrieked in horror. Diving into the minds of the dead was no piece of cake, but it was a whole hell of a lot easier than placing a soul back in a body.

"Stay focused," Gideon whispered as he wrapped his free arm around my waist so I didn't fall. "You're stronger than you know."

"Baby's okay?" I gasped out.

"The child is stronger than both of us. She's fine."

I decided to believe him. The alternative would be devastating. My body convulsed in agony as the soul glimmered and dissolved into June's chest. I didn't remove my hand from her cheek. My gut and my heart told me staying physically connected to June was the key. My survival instincts told me to run like hell. I ignored them. The air was being squeezed and stolen from my lungs. Black spots raced across my vision. Thousands of needles pricked at my skin. I held on.

I refused to let go.

Charlie's grip on my hand tightened. Under normal circumstances it would have hurt. The circumstances were not normal. I squeezed back. Something snapped. Unsure if it was my bones or his, I paid no attention. Bones could heal. There was no healing June if this didn't work.

"Too much," I choked out, keeping my hand on June's cheek with an effort that I was sure was going to kill me. "It's too much."

"Scream," Heather insisted. "Let it out."

The permission was so cathartic, I almost cried.

I didn't. I screamed.

I screamed with fury at the vicious pain racking my body.

I screamed for the gross injustice that had been done to June by Clarissa.

I screamed out the sadness I felt at Steve's departure into the light.

I screamed at the truth that my mother had been murdered by Clarissa.

I screamed with hatred at the Angels who had left my father and me to die by Clarissa's hand.

They had failed.

I had no plans to do the same.

Golden crystals rained down from the ceiling and scattered across the bed and hardwood floor. A spring-scented wind blew through the room, mixing with the crystals and making it difficult to see. The pain in my body was replaced by a feeling of anticipation so strong, I thought I might float away on the breeze. Only Gideon's touch kept me grounded in reality.

The sound of a beating heart echoed in my ears and grew louder with each passing second. Candy Vargo continued to sing. The melody got swept up in the wind, and the swirling breeze sounded like an eerie accompaniment.

It was beautiful.

My hand on June's cheek didn't feel like it belonged to me. It belonged to something much larger and far more important. Closing my eyes, I simply breathed into all the emotions dancing through me.

And then everything stopped. The wind abated. Candy Vargo stopped singing. The crystals ceased to fall from the ceiling. The silence was as loud as an explosion.

Too terrified to open my eyes, I eased my hand from June's cheek and waited.

"Holy shit on a fuckin' stick," Candy Vargo grunted.

"Oh my God," Heather muttered.

"Did it work?" I whispered with my eyes still tightly shut.

"And then some," Gram said, sounding shocked.

"Charlie?" June asked groggily.

"I'm here, June," he said in a voice clogged with raw emotion. "And so are you."

I'd never heard such beautiful words in my entire forty years. My body tingled and sagged with intense relief. If Gideon didn't have a grip on me, I would have dropped to the ground like a sack of potatoes.

"Wow," my mom said. "I'm not sure…"

"She's alive," my father said firmly. "That's all that matters."

Hang on. While Charlie's words were encouraging, no one else's words were. Did I give her two heads? Was she deformed? Had I ruined one of my best friends?

"Open your eyes, Daisy," Gideon urged.

Slowly, I followed his direction. My lashes were caked with crystals, and I was sure what I saw was wrong. It was impossible.

June was beautiful, but she wasn't exactly the June I remembered.

Wait. *Nothing* was impossible.

"Umm, Charlie?" I asked, wildly concerned. "How exactly did you picture June?"

Charlie looked as surprised and alarmed as everyone else. "You weren't specific."

"Mmkay," I said, trying to figure out what we were supposed to do now. "While that may be true, can you answer my question?"

Charlie cleared his throat, then scrubbed his hands over his face. "I pictured her as the woman I fell in love with all those years ago."

I nodded slowly. "So… umm… you pictured June at what age?"

"Twenty-five," he whispered so softly, I barely heard him.

"Well, that makes sense," Candy said with a chuckle. "Gonna be kinda hard to explain though."

"Understatement," Heather said under her breath.

"What happened?" June asked, sitting up and looking around the room. "Did I faint?"

I exchanged a quick glance with Gideon, who was as perplexed as I was. Sitting down on the edge of the bed, I gently brushed June's hair out of her face. "Do you remember anything?" I asked.

She stared at me for a long moment, then shook her head. "No, I don't. I'm so sorry. Did I ruin the luncheon?"

"No," I told her, unsure what to do.

Charlie saved me. "If everyone could leave June and me alone, that would be helpful."

"Not a problem," Heather said, grabbing Missy's hand and hightailing it out of the room.

My father nodded. He quietly left with the ghosts of my mom and Gram following. The Tasmanian Devil and her cohorts silently faded away. Gideon touched my shoulder and gave it a slight squeeze.

"Remember, the truth works the best," Candy Vargo warned Charlie. "You're not God. Don't be making no rules for anybody or bending reality." Shoving a toothpick into her mouth, she walked out of the room.

"Daisy," June said, shaking her head in confusion. "I feel like…"

"What?" I asked with a smile, trying not to gape at the twenty-five-year-old version of my fifty-seven-year-old friend.

"I don't know," she said with a confused giggle. "I just don't know."

"That's okay, June." I leaned over and kissed her cheek

the same way I'd done when she'd been on the edge of death.

She touched her cheek and smiled absently. "My goodness, I think I had the strangest dreams."

"We'll be downstairs if you need us," I said, taking Gideon's hand and turning to leave the room. I didn't trust myself to keep acting normal. June didn't need me to stare openmouthed at her.

Charlie smiled at me. His joy was visceral. I felt it all the way to my toes. I had no clue how he and June were going to go forward, but it was now in his court.

"Didn't expect that," Gideon said as we descended the stairs.

"Nope," I agreed. "They have kids older than June. Not sure how that's going to work out."

"They might have to move away—start a new life," Gideon said. "Possibly have to stage their own deaths."

The thought stopped me dead in my tracks. "That will be awful for them. June worships her kids and grandkids."

Gideon ran his hands through his hair. "I don't see a way around it. Charlie can easily age himself to match June and they can be together."

"Is June Immortal now?" I asked, feeling wonky. I wasn't sure trading death for Immortality was a good plan for her. "Will she age?"

"Remains to be seen." Gideon shrugged. "None of us have ever witnessed anything like it. I have nothing to base an assumption on."

Had I played God? Did I hurt June more than I may have helped her?

"Daisy," Gideon said, putting his hand under my chin and raising my gaze to his. "Stop. Do not go there. Regret is a waste of time. June's life was stolen by a monstrosity. You gave June and Charlie a gift that can't be repaid. It's on Charlie as to how June came back. He'll have to figure it out."

I nodded. "That's huge," I said.

"Correct. However, not so long ago you knew nothing about any of this," he pointed out. "You're doing fine."

I raised a brow and grinned. "Define fine."

Gideon laughed. His laugh made everything alright in my world. I craved the sound. He placed his hand on my stomach and gazed into my eyes.

"I love you, Daisy Leigh Amara-Jones. I'm besotted with the life we created inside you. As Charlie wisely said, love is an intangible emotion that words don't suffice in describing," he said, making my heart skip a beat or three. "It's invisible—weighs nothing. However, it's stronger than any magic I've come across in my millions of years. You're my addiction and my meaning, Daisy. You're the person I was destined to find."

Throwing my arms around him and almost making us tumble down the stairs, I kissed him. "Actions speak louder than words," I whispered. "And yes. I am fine."

Gideon gave me a naughty lopsided smirk. "Fine you are," he agreed, copping a feel of my bottom. "Very, very fine."

I rolled my eyes and grinned. "You're not too bad yourself, Reaper."

"Thank you, Counselor," he said, then paused. "Or rather, Angel."

I wrinkled my nose. "We're gonna need to discuss that."

"It can be arranged," he agreed. "How about this evening? I want to take you somewhere."

I liked the sound of that. "Works for me. Let's go make sure everyone is okay. I'm worried about Jennifer too."

"Never a dull moment," he said, taking my hand.

"You got that right."

CHAPTER THREE

"I BEG YOUR PARDON?" TIM DEMANDED, VERY PALE AND ON the verge of passing out.

Candy Vargo shrugged and plopped her feet on my coffee table. "June looks about fourteen. Gonna be a problem. Lips'll start flappin' in town if Charlie's banging a teenager. He'll get his ass thrown in the pokey."

I rolled my eyes as I crossed the room and knocked her dirty tennis-shoe-clad feet off the table. "Candy, for the love of everything stupid and wildly inappropriate, you need to shut your cakehole. That's not true, and it's mean to freak Tim out like that."

"Payback's a bitch," Gram warned Candy, shaking a ghostly finger at her. "If you keep yappin', you better give your heart to Jesus, 'cause that butt is mine."

"Fine," Candy grumbled. "None of you people can take a joke."

"A joke is funny," Heather pointed out, giving Candy the stink eye. "That was not."

"So, June doesn't look fourteen?" Tim asked, still unsure what to believe. "Fifteen then?"

He was a very literal guy.

"She looks twenty-five," I told him. "Still a problem, but not as severe as Candy wanted you to believe."

Tim was intrigued. Sitting down on the couch next to Heather and Missy, he pulled a pad of paper and a pen from the pocket of his mail carrier uniform.

"This is quite unusual. It makes me wonder if reintroducing the soul back into the body undid the normal aging process in the human gene activity," he mused aloud as he jotted down notes. "It's been tested in research with mice—not the reintroduction of the soul but reverse aging experiments."

"That's human science," my dad said. "What was done was not science."

"True that," Candy agreed. "Wasn't real human either."

"Which begs another question," Missy said. "Is June human anymore?"

My father sighed. "That's the ten-thousand-dollar question. The answer is, none of us know."

"Correct," Tim said, still jotting away. "However, June's blood can be tested for abnormalities and we can observe if she leaves a footprint."

"All Immortals have a footprint?" Missy asked.

Missy was the only human in the room aside from me. Mom and Gram were human but they were also dead so it didn't technically count. Although, I wasn't sure *what* I was at the moment. What I did know was that I didn't have a footprint, which meant I wasn't Immortal.

Gideon nodded. "They do. All Immortals leave one, so to speak."

"And it looks like a regular footprint?" Missy asked.

"Looks different to all of us," Candy Vargo explained. "Charlie sees shadows. Gideon senses them. I feel a tingle in my left knocker. It's the bigger boob."

"Candy Vargo," Gram yelled, zipping across the room. "You need to quit tellin' crappy jokes. And for the record, your right knocker is bigger, not the left."

Candy glanced down at her chest in shock. "I think you're correct. Well, I'll be damned."

"Pretty sure you already are," Heather told her. "And Gram, Candy isn't joking. Her *knockers* tingle when she spots a footprint."

Gram's brows shot up and she cackled. "My apologies, Candy. But I'm still goin' on record that the right one is bigger than the left."

"Candy Vargo's *knockers* aside, we do have a problem," Heather said, running her hands through her sleek pixie cut.

"What can be done for June?" my mom asked, sitting next to my dad on the overstuffed armchair. Part of her semi-transparent body melted into his. I was aware neither of them could feel each other, but I loved seeing them together.

"They could leave," my dad said. "Charlie can age himself backward to June's age and they can start over somewhere else."

"I thought the same," Gideon said. "Their children are

the issue and, of course, the fact that they're known here in town."

Heather blew out a long, slow breath. "June will freak."

I nodded and sat down on the arm of the chair next to my parents. "She may have no choice. Gideon said they could stage their deaths."

"I can do that," Candy volunteered gleefully. Violence and death were her thing. "What do we want? An explosion? Sky diving accident? Hit and run?"

I winced. The conversation was getting morbid, and that was rich coming from me, considering I counseled the dead. "How about we let them decide?"

"How about I just fix it?" Tim suggested.

All eyes shot to Tim.

"How?" Gideon asked.

Tim smiled. It was incredibly naughty and very cute. However, I knew something unsettling was about to happen.

"Candy, may I?" he inquired.

Candy's eyes narrowed to slits. "May you what?"

"Use you as an experiment," Tim replied innocently.

"For?" she demanded.

"For all the times you skipped out on paying your half of the check in the last ninety or so years. For the time you ran over me with a chariot and I lost both of my legs. For the time you made me eat Pop Rocks and Mentos then drink a soda at the opera. Shall I go on?"

"That was hilarious," Candy commented with a grin.

Tim wasn't grinning. I had no clue what he had planned, but it was clear he needed some help convincing Candy.

"What about the time you got yourself decapitated so you would know what it felt like?" I asked, tattling on her, fully knowing Gram would blow a gasket.

"You did WHAT?" Gram bellowed.

Daisy for the win.

Candy blanched in terror.

"Candy Vargo," Gram yelled in her outdoor voice. "That ain't a proper thing for a lady to do. The toothpicks, the f-bombs, the hairy legs, and now I find out you got your dadgum head cut off on purpose? I just don't know what to do with you. I should jerk you up and tie your tail in a dang knot. You best not remove your noggin ever again. Am I clear?"

"Yes, ma'am," Candy said sheepishly with a tiny smile pulling at her lips.

Gram was loud. She had been loud in life. She was loud in death. And she was loud in love. She loved Candy Vargo, and Candy Vargo adored being loved by Gram.

"You go on and let Tim do what he needs to do," Gram told her. "That Mentos thing was just plain rude."

"The chariot thing wasn't real good either," Missy pointed out.

Candy rolled her eyes. "Everyone needs to relax their cracks. His legs grew back."

"Umm… not exactly the point," I said, slightly unable to believe the direction the conversation had taken.

Candy thought about it and picked her teeth until she caught Gram's disapproving glare. Quickly shoving the toothpick between the cushions on the couch, she swore and nodded her head at Tim. "Fine," she consented. "But if it hurts, you're gonna have to watch your back for the next decade or two."

"Rephrase that bullcrap," Gram admonished her. "And remove that wooden spit stick from Daisy's couch. Your manners are givin' me gas and that's impossible since I'm dead, girlie."

With a huge put-upon sigh and a not-so-secret smile, Candy dug for the toothpick and put it in her pocket. I was pretty sure she would use it again, which was gross and vintage Candy Vargo. Eyeing Tim warily, she pointed at him. "Is this gonna help June?"

"I do believe it will," Tim announced, putting his notebook down and standing up. After cracking his knuckles, he did a few deep knee bends then rolled his neck.

"Shit," Heather said, grabbing Missy and pulling her away from whatever the hell was about to go down.

"Can I ask what you're going to do?" I questioned. Immortals seemed oblivious to collateral damage. While Gideon and I were going to build a new home together, I loved my old farmhouse. It would suck if Tim blew it up.

"Since June is still somewhat human, I need to practice a little something on Candy Vargo," he said.

"Don't make sense," Gram pointed out. "If whatever voodoo you're gonna do on Candy works, don't mean it will work on June."

"Fine point. Well made," Tim replied. "However, I will place money that June is no longer *completely* human. If I'm correct in my assumption, the spell I will cast won't harm her. However, I haven't cast this particular hex in several centuries. Candy is the perfect guinea pig since killing her is an impossibility."

"Gideon, Clarence and Heather can't die," Candy griped. "Why do I have to be the pig?"

"Guinea pig," Tim corrected her. "Clarence, Gideon and Heather never forced me to eat Pop Rocks and Mentos then drink a soda… at the opera… in the front row."

"Oh my God," Missy said, trying not to laugh. "That's awful."

"Word," I muttered then got to an important point as far as the future of my home was

concerned. "Should we do this outside?"

Tim considered my question as we all stared at him. When he wasn't forthcoming with an answer, I kept talking.

"I like my house," I told him. "I'd really hate for it to blow up. Plus, Missy, Jennifer and I are human, and possibly June. So, it could be a seriously bad plan to incinerate the farmhouse considering a few of us might not live through it. You feel me?"

Tim smiled and nodded. "I completely understand," he assured me. "There's no fire involved and nothing will be detonated. You have my word."

"Okay," I said, hoping I hadn't left out something that could end with me being homeless. Tim was painfully literal.

"Just do it," Candy griped. "I don't like being in suspense, dumbass."

"As you wish," Tim replied, waving his hand in Candy Vargo's direction.

Tim was as good as his word. There was only a small

pop of green and silver light as he cast the spell. No fire. No explosions. The farmhouse was in one piece.

"Oh my God," Heather wheezed, laughing so hard she had to bend over.

"Fascinating," my dad said with a chuckle.

"Amazing," my mother added with a giggle.

I was speechless. Missy was laughing with Heather. Gideon raised a brow and grinned. Gram was simply in shock.

And Tim? Tim was preening.

"Fuck all of you asshats," Candy shouted, glancing down at herself in horror. "You better be able to reverse this shit, mail boy."

The language was pure Candy Vargo. However, the foul words were being spit out by a ten-year-old version of the Keeper of Fate. She was actually adorable—extremely potty-mouthed, but very cute.

"Wow," I said, trying to bite back my grin. Candy was pissed. When she was pissed, she was violent. While Tim's spell didn't take down my house, her hissy fit might. "How long will it last?"

Tim checked his watch. "About six hours, give or take."

"No can do," little Candy snapped, standing up and tripping over her now too large sweatpants. "You switch me back now or I will short sheet your bed for a decade and cut holes in all your underpants. You hear me?"

"Can't," Tim said, gleefully dodging an irate miniature Candy, who was trying to tackle him.

"Watch out," Gideon said with a chuckle as he pulled me out of the fray. "She might be ten but she's still dangerous."

"Enough," Gram shouted as Candy dove at Tim and tried to bite him. "We're gonna use this as a learning experience."

Candy stomped her foot and glared at Gram.

Gram crossed her arms over her chest and glared right back. "You wipe that nasty look off your face right now, or I'm gonna wipe it off for you after I whoop your ass."

"You can't," Candy told her triumphantly.

Candy had a point. Gram was a ghost.

"Metaphorically speaking," my mom said, floating over next to Gram in solidarity. "And trust me, real or not, you don't want a Gram whooping."

Candy considered her options carefully as Tim hid behind a chair. "Define a fucking learning experience."

It was kind of horrible to hear the f-bomb fly out of a ten-year-old's mouth, but it was also hilarious considering the source.

"You never got the right trainin'," Gram said, shaking her head at the potty language. "Now that you're a youngin' we can start you over."

"For six hours," Heather chimed in, still laughing.

"Put a cork in it, Arbitrator," Candy hissed.

"My bad," Heather replied, grinning. "But you are super cute."

Candy's eyes narrowed as she glanced over at Gram.

"That was a compliment," Gram warned. "What do you say to someone when they say somethin' nice?"

"Fuck you?" Candy asked seriously.

"Hell to the no!" Gram shouted. "Put on a jacket. We're headin' outside for some etiquette lessons."

"Coat's gonna be too big," Candy bitched, rolling up her sweatpants.

"Too bad, so sad," Gram said. "Alana, you wanna help your mama knock some manners into Candy Vargo?"

"I most certainly do," my mom said. "But I think hugging is far better than knocking."

Gram winked at her. "As do I. Move that foul-mouthed little butt, Candy. We've got work to do."

Candy pulled on her oversized coat and walked out of the house like she was walking into the bowels of Hell. Gram and Mom followed her with smiles on their faces. My dogs Donna and Karen trailed them as well. They were always up for an outside adventure.

"In all my life, I never ever thought I would see that," Heather said, watching them out of the bay window.

"Candy loves it," I said, joining her and watching Gram make Candy curtsey. The dogs barked happily and zoomied all over the yard.

"That she does," my dad said with a smile. "Being loved is rare."

Gideon shot me a glance and a smile. We were two of the rare lucky ones. He turned his attention to Tim, who was still hiding. "You believe that could work on June? You can set the correct age?"

Standing up warily and staying far from the front door just in case Candy came charging back in to retaliate, Tim nodded. "I do. It could solve a multitude of issues for June and Charlie. They might have to limit their time with their children, but I am confident it can work."

I squinted at Tim. "So, you made Candy Vargo ten years old on purpose?"

Tim giggled. "I did."

"You're bad," I told him with a grin.

"Actually, he's damn good," Heather contradicted. "Candy might act pissed, but she's having the time of her life out there being fussed over by Gram and Alana."

Candy was all smiles as she watched Alana show her how to sit on a chair properly. Gram clapped like a fool when Candy finally sat down without her legs splayed wide open. Little Candy blushed with the praise.

"Unreal," I whispered with a laugh. "Does anyone think the etiquette lessons will stick?"

"My guess would be no," Gideon surmised. "But that would be because she wants more of Gram's attention."

"Gram gives excellent attention," I said. "My life was better for it."

"Daisy?" Jennifer asked, walking into the living room with a dazed expression on her face.

Oh my God, I'd forgotten about her. "Hey," I said, moving quickly across the room and leading her to the couch. "You okay?"

She scratched her head. "Not sure. I must of drank a shit-ton of wine. Feel kinda like I blacked out."

"Sleeping it off was smart," I said, hoping Charlie and the twenty-five-year-old June didn't decide to come down the stairs right now.

"I think I better be gettin' home," she said. "Are June and Charlie still here? He dropped us off."

"I'll drive you home," Tim offered. "They left a while ago."

Jennifer gave Tim a weak thumbs up. "Thanks. I had the strangest dreams. I just can't shake feeling like all you folks are vampires." She laughed at the absurdity.

We laughed, but it was forced.

"Just nuts," she said as she found her purse and coat. "Coulda sworn there was a bodyless hand too. Never gonna mix red and white again."

"Crap," Heather muttered under her breath, wiggling her fingers and restoring the front yard back to its former state before the shitshow had destroyed it this morning. That would confuse Jennifer even more.

"Should we let her leave?" I whispered to Gideon.

"Not sure," Gideon replied. "But it's safer for her not to see June right now."

"Agreed," Clarence said quietly, coming up behind us.

"She probably shouldn't be alone," I said.

My father nodded. "Tim, I believe it would be wise to stay with Jennifer until she feels better."

Tim saluted my dad and offered his arm to Jennifer. "I will make sure my dear friend is in good shape."

"That's real sweet of you," Jennifer told him. "Dip won't be back from the police retreat for a few days. We can have a fun evening—do face masks and look up trivia to gross everybody out. Sound good?"

"Sweeter words have never been spoken," Tim replied with delight. "I shall endeavor to find the most appalling facts known to man."

"Awesome," I said, walking them to the door. "Lunch here tomorrow. No wine."

Jennifer groaned. "I'm teetotalin' it for a while. I've got a mother-humper of a hangover."

Gram and Alana quickly directed Candy to hide as Jennifer and Tim walked out of the front door. Seating Jennifer in his mail truck, Tim covertly waved to Candy. She flipped him off.

"Is it possible Jennifer remembers?" Heather asked as we watched them drive away.

"I wouldn't think so," Gideon said. "However, it certainly seems like she does—at least partially."

"I find that very difficult to believe," my dad said. "Those Angels are very powerful."

Heather rolled her eyes. "*Those Angels* are your children."

Clarence's expression turned hard and his eyes blazed gold. My dad was a badass and forgetting that would be a grave mistake. The Archangel Michael didn't suffer fools. "I have two children—Daisy and you. *Those Angels* may carry my DNA, but they are no children of mine."

There was a long and uncomfortable silence. I was aware I would have to deal with my despicable siblings since they'd called a tribunal on me for killing Clarissa, but I'd leave thinking about that disaster until tomorrow. The events of today had been more than enough.

"Breakfast for dinner?" Gideon suggested. "I can make pancakes."

Gideon's pancakes were heavenly. During his incomprehensibly long life, he'd been to culinary school. The Grim

Reaper's list of accomplishments was long and impressive. His hobby over many decades had been getting degrees. He'd been a lawyer, a doctor, a social worker, a human rights activist, professor of philosophy, firefighter, a sculptor, and the list went on and on. Of course, it tickled me to no end that one of his favorite professions was a dog trainer. The man with the bad reputation was actually a very good person.

"I'm starving," Heather said. "I'll make eggs while you whip up pancakes."

"Daisy, do you have oranges?" Missy asked.

"I do," I replied, realizing I was ravenous.

"I'll make juice," she volunteered, then winked at me. "You're eating for two, gotta keep you healthy."

I stared down at my flat stomach in wonder. Missy was correct. I was now eating for two. For today being one of the worst days of my life thus far, it was also one of the best.

Life was back to normal—as long as the definition of normal was abnormal.

CHAPTER FOUR

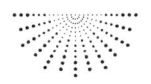

THE KITCHEN WAS THE HEART OF MY FARMHOUSE—WARM AND inviting with a well-used and loved large oak kitchen table. The median age of the people around it at the moment was a number I couldn't fathom. However, it was strangely perfect. My dead houseguests floated around with excitement and chattered unintelligibly at my live guests. The Tasmanian Devil had terrified everyone a few times, popping out of random drawers and the fridge. At one point, my dad got so spooked by her, he accidently let loose with a blast of magic and blew up the toaster. I laughed. My sense of humor had either evolved or warped—both descriptions worked.

When life was crazy, one either joined in or freaked out. I'd joined in with a vengeance and wasn't looking back.

Gideon's pancakes were amazing as usual. Heather had made a platter of fluffy scrambled eggs, and Missy had squeezed enough pulpy orange juice for an army. Before the toaster had bitten the dust, my dad had toasted an entire loaf of bread while my mom and Gram had directed him on buttering it. We had duly accomplished the Southern requirement of making way too much food.

My home was filled with people—dead and alive—who I loved. And the conversation was bizarre, lively and profanely violent thanks to Candy Vargo.

"If you keep staring at me, I'm gonna plant my fork in your forehead," Candy warned Heather as she shoved pancakes into her mouth like she hadn't eaten in a week.

Candy Vargo—still an adorable ten-year-old version of herself—had done nothing to help with the meal, which was probably a good thing. However, she'd placed a pile of toothpicks on the table for after-dinner use. I hoped they weren't *already* used, but knowing Candy, they most likely were.

Heather laughed. "Try it," she taunted Candy. "I'll break your scrawny little body in half like a twig."

"Goddangit," Gram grumbled, shaking her head as she floated in the air over the table. "You people are violent. First off, there will be no stabbin' and no breakin'. Am I clear, ladies?"

Heather smiled and nodded at Gram. Candy flipped Heather off then looked to Gram for approval. She didn't get it. It was rather disconcerting to see a child flip off an adult.

Gram rolled her eyes. "You're a hot mess, Candy Vargo. I'm gonna have to double down on the lessons."

"Well, shit," Candy grunted. "Lemme get this straight. Are you sayin' it's not good to flip the bird at a jackhole even when they deserve to have their entrails ripped out? I mean, I can see how forking Heather in the head while other people are eating might be a bad move. While syrup is delicious on pancakes, fuckin' blood is not."

Gram stared at Candy with her mouth wide open. Even Gram was left speechless by Candy Vargo.

I stepped in before Candy kept waxing graphically and grossly poetic. "No stabbing. No flipping. No entrail removing. Basically, nothing that makes people bleed."

Candy took it all in. "Flippin' the bird isn't bloody," she pointed out.

"Good God," Gram shouted. "I'm movin' in with you, Candy Vargo. I didn't realize the dang crisis that we had on our hands."

Candy paled. "You're what?"

"Movin' in," Gram repeated. "You need twenty-four-seven supervision."

Little Candy Vargo was appalled. "But…"

"No buts," Gram snapped. "You finish up your supper and we're goin' home."

"Umm… my house is a little messy," Candy admitted.

"When's the last time you cleaned?" my mom asked her.

Candy Vargo was stumped. She had no clue. That didn't bode well.

Gram threw her hands in the air. "Well, I guess you're gonna be moppin' and dustin' for a week, girlie."

"Or a month," Heather added.

Candy held up her fork and aimed it at Heather. I immediately removed the weapon from her hand. She just shrugged and continued to eat with her fingers.

"Moving on," my dad said with a smile as he and Gideon began to clear the plates. "Did Charlie answer the door when you brought up food?"

"No," I told him. "I knocked lightly and let them know I was leaving a tray and some clean clothes for June." I paused and ran my hands through my hair. "I think I heard June crying."

"It's a lot to absorb," Heather said.

"Understatement," I agreed. It had taken me a while to believe I wasn't insane. It was anyone's guess to figure out how June would handle all the *impossible that wasn't impossible*.

"Do you want us to stay?" Heather asked.

"Yes," Gideon said before I could answer. "Daisy and I need to talk, and I want to get her away from here for a few hours. I'd appreciate it very much if you stayed while we're gone."

I blushed as Missy winked at me. Gideon had basically implied that we were getting away to *get busy*. Whatever. I hoped we were. Although, we did have some talking to do.

"Get a move on, Vargo," Gram ordered. "I'm ready to see that messy house of yours."

Candy stood up and burped loudly. She shoved a toothpick into her mouth, covertly flipped off a grinning Heather and walked out of the kitchen holding her ten-year-old head high.

"Gram, don't be too hard on her," I said with a grin.

Gram chuckled. "That girl is happier than Karen and Donna layin' on the front porch eatin' a big old catfish head. Candy Vargo might think I'm gonna slap her to sleep then slap her for sleepin', but she knows I love her and her foul mouth. Ain't nobody ever gave a damn for that one. I plan to make up for it."

On that loving yet terrifying note, Gram flew out of the room. Candy was going to experience Gram love in a big way.

"Good luck to Gram," Heather said with a laugh. "She's going to need it."

My mom smiled. "Gram doesn't need luck. She needs Candy as much as Candy needs her. My mother loves having someone to fuss over and boss around. And Candy Vargo is ripe for a good bossing."

"True," I said with a grin, remembering all the times growing up when Gram had let me know the way it was going to be in her outdoor voice. She loved with passion and with lung power. Wiping down the table, I pushed the past away and focused on the now. "Do you think Charlie and June will even come down tonight?"

"Not a clue," my father replied, carefully turning on the dishwasher while keeping an eye out for the Tasmanian Devil. The ghost was a flying horror show.

Glancing around, I watched as Gideon dried platters with a dishtowel and Heather wrapped up the leftovers. I smiled. It was odd to see people who could snap their fingers and clean up a mess doing it the old-fashioned human way. However, I'd witnessed enough magic today and was grateful for the mundane.

"Should we stay as well?" my mom inquired, floating over to my dad and inspecting his outstanding cleaning job.

"Go home," Heather insisted. "Missy and I will stay until

Gideon and Daisy get back. If it's too late, we'll crash in a guest room."

"June might want to talk," I pointed out. "Might be better if you just plan on staying the night."

Heather nodded. "You're right. We'll stay." She looked over at Missy.

"Agreed," Missy said. "You guys go *talk*."

Gideon raised a brow and eyed Missy. "We *are* going to talk."

"Right," Missy said, waggling her brows. "Have fun with that, dude."

Gideon stood in the middle of the kitchen, unsure what to do. Being teased by friends wasn't exactly normal for him. He was the Grim Reaper. I was pretty sure he didn't have many friends.

"She's playing with you," I told him quickly. "Do not electrocute my best friend. You're gonna have to get used to it."

Gideon laughed. The sound made me tingle. His existence had been very bleak at times, but that was his lot in life. Our future was bright.

I hoped.

"Got it," he said, folding the dish towel then grabbing my hand and pulling me to my feet. "No electrocuting friends. I can work with that."

"Good to know," Heather said, shooting him a glare. If anyone harmed a hair on Missy's head, Heather would go apeshit on them.

"I'd suggest leaving before your lack of human social skills gets you into more trouble," my father advised

Gideon. "I do believe this is one of the longer spans of time you've spent in this realm in quite a while."

My stomach tightened. Pressing my lips together, I held back the millions of questions that blasted through my head. A span of time to someone who had lived forever could be hundreds of years... thousands of years. Did Gideon have to go back to the darkness? Was that in the job description? Would I be raising our daughter by myself?

"We're leaving. Now," Gideon stated firmly, recognizing my tension. "Shall we drive?"

I nodded. "Yep. I need normal right now. No transporting."

"Your wish is my command."

～

THE NIGHT WAS COLD AND THE SKY WAS FULL OF LOW-hanging stars. They were so bright it may as well have been daytime. The drive had been silent with both of us lost in our own thoughts. After a short hike, we now stood in the middle of the starlit field where I'd recently been *trained* by my friends to protect myself from Clarissa. While the field had been full of violence during my lessons—albeit friendly violence, for lack of a better way to describe it—it was now serene and beautiful.

"I love it here," I said quietly.

"Me too," Gideon replied. "Almost as much as I love you."

"Cheesy," I said with a laugh.

He grinned. "Definitely, but I stand by my words."

Gideon had purchased the gorgeous piece of property

for us. He had a home in town and I had the farmhouse, but we wanted something that was ours together. The Grim Reaper owned property all over the world. I'd suggested he pare that down. There were only so many houses a person could actually live in. He'd agreed but was keeping his place in Greece. I was cool with that, seeing as how visiting Greece was on my bucket list.

We'd already laid our metaphorical foundation and now it was time to make it real. The thought of living together thrilled me. It was a huge step, but we'd already jumped off the cliff and made a baby. Making a home together felt natural and right.

Wrapping my head around the fact that I was carrying our child was surreal. My mind raced with joy and fear. I was only forty. Plenty of women had children in their forties. However, no woman I knew had a partner who'd been around since the beginning of time. Making an appointment with my gynecologist was on the top of my never-ending list. Although, I should probably check with Charlie on that. If our daughter's DNA was wonked due to her *unusual* parentage, that could be an issue and create problems we didn't need.

"It's time to build our home," Gideon said, taking my hand in his. "Tell me what you want."

It was such a loaded question.

"I want you to tell me that you'll stay with me while I'm alive," I whispered.

Gideon inhaled sharply. He said nothing.

"You can't tell me that," I said, my stomach sinking.

"I can tell you that I want to," he replied carefully.

"Nothing is guaranteed except the moment we're in."

"Not exactly what I want to hear."

"Not exactly what I want to say," he replied, looking up at the stars. He expelled a long, slow breath then turned his gaze on me. It was filled with love, desire and wonder. "I can promise if I have to leave, I will always come back to you. Always."

I nodded curtly and sucked back the need to cry. He was giving me everything he had to give. Crying or begging would change nothing. My feelings for the man standing next to me were so large, there weren't enough words to describe them.

"All right," I said, releasing his hand and pacing to get my chaotic thoughts in order. "I don't want to talk about that anymore. Next subject. You're really okay with us being pregnant?"

"*Okay* is too mild of a word," he replied, unable to stop the wide grin that pulled at his lips. "Never in my existence did I think I would have any of this. I'm not sure you can understand—not sure I can explain it."

"Try," I said.

His smile grew even wider. "At the risk of sounding cheesy again, which I embrace with no embarrassment… When you live forever, physical and spiritual existence cease to have meaning. What one might find gratifying, amusing, diverting and entertaining no longer holds any appeal. The world becomes colorless and void of anything that makes sense. You're my color—my meaning… my reason. And Mini-Daisy is an unimaginable gift I don't deserve."

"So that's a yes?" I asked with a laugh.

"Unequivocally."

"Good to know," I told him, feeling light-headed with joy. "And for the record, her name will *not* be Mini-Daisy."

"It's a very good name," he pointed out. "It's my favorite name. And I don't think Gideonia has a good ring to it."

"Oh my God," I said with a giggle. "Gideonia is awful."

His cheesiness was sexy. Everything about him was sexy.

"Fine point. Well made," he replied with a wink. "We can discuss names soon."

"Deal," I said, knowing I already had a name in mind. But we were talking and I had more questions for the man I loved to the point of ridiculousness. "Are we going to have fights?"

Gideon looked perplexed. "I would guess so. Most couples do from what I understand. However, I vow to put the toilet seat down and not squeeze the toothpaste from the top. I also do dishes."

"Not what I meant," I said, shaking my head and smiling. "You're the Grim Reaper. I'm now the Angel of Mercy. Seems like our jobs might butt heads."

Gideon snapped his fingers and an ornate, cushioned bench appeared next to a blazing firepit. I marveled at how magic seemed normal to me now. I was cold. The fire was welcome no matter how it had been built.

"Sit with me, Daisy," he said, extending his hand.

His beauty was absurd and still made me catch my breath. I did as requested and cuddled up to his huge, warm body. His scent and physical closeness calmed me. His body relaxed as I burrowed even closer.

"Most souls are already destined to their appropriate afterlife when the time arrives," he said, playing with my wild dark hair. "It's unusual and uncommon that a soul's fate is in question."

Glancing up at him, I squinted. "You've never had to determine the fate of a soul?"

"Not what I said," he replied. "But it's only happened a handful of times."

"And who won?" I asked. "You or Clarissa?"

I hated even saying the woman's name. Her self-assigned mission had been to destroy me and in some ways she'd succeeded. However, in the end she'd paid. Of course, now I was in trouble for ending her life, but I would do it again in a heartbeat. I was sure the visiting Angels would show their hand soon. The fact that I was technically related to them was alarming. Unfortunately, I didn't see that as working to my advantage.

"It's not so much winning as it is determining," Gideon explained. "No soul is flawless and without sin. Very little in life is black and white. Shades of gray are what most of us are made of."

"Got it," I said. "You didn't answer my question."

Immortals were cryptic and tended to skirt around issues. My father was the champion of omission.

Gideon raised a brow and smiled. "You're awfully pushy."

"Yep. I come by it honestly. I was raised by Gram. I have big lady balls. Answer me, please."

"Fifty-fifty," he said. "Although, there was agreement on both sides."

I found that a little difficult to believe. Clarissa hadn't been what I would call reasonable. Gideon chuckled at my incredulous expression. He could read me like a book.

"She wasn't always the way she was in the end," he explained with a tired sigh. He didn't enjoy talking about the monster any more than I did. It sucked but was unavoidable. Even in death she was still hanging around.

I had Clarissa's job now, plus my own as the Death Counselor. I didn't want to be the Angel of Mercy, but June's life was more important than what I wanted. Hell, I didn't even know the position's requirements… and I was pretty sure there wasn't a company handbook.

"So, Clarissa was *nice* at one time?" I asked.

"Nice would be a stretch," Gideon admitted. "However, she wasn't always as insanely unbalanced as she'd become."

I absorbed the information and decided that I would cross each bridge as it came. A game without rules would be difficult to explain or understand. And honestly, my brain was full right now. Defining something that was a moving target would be an effort in futility.

"Moving on," I said, realizing I sounded like my dad. "What kind of house do you want?"

Gideon grinned and slashed his hand through the crisp evening air. "I was thinking something like this."

Before my eyes, a breathtaking home appeared. It wasn't much bigger than my farmhouse, which was perfect. I didn't want to live in a grand mansion like the one my father had built to hide my mother and their relationship from Clarissa.

"Holy cow." I giggled as I stood up to get a better look. "Did you dive into my mind?"

"I did not," Gideon said with mock offense. "I just think I have a good idea of what you like."

"Nailed it," I replied.

The graceful lines of the house were charming. It had a Cape Cod feel but was two stories instead of one. The gray-blue cedar shingle exterior was trimmed in white and the steep, slate-black gabled roof was so pretty. Gideon had taken liberties with the style that I heartily approved of. He'd added a wraparound porch that begged for rocking chairs and a swing. The front door was flanked by paned windows and the symmetrical lines of the structure spoke to my soul.

Enchanting dormers popped out of the roof and a large slate-gray stone chimney sat nestled between them. It was every kind of perfect.

"You like?" he asked.

"I love," I replied. "Is it furnished inside?"

"Only two rooms," he said with a lopsided grin.

"Let me guess," I said, my smile matching his. "The master bedroom?"

"But of course," he replied with a smile hot enough to melt my panties.

"And the other?"

"Let me show you," he said, looking a little unsure of himself.

His lack of confidence was odd. I'd never seen him apprehensive. Whatever he'd done inside the house, I would love it… even if I didn't.

"It's okay if you hate it," he said, not making eye contact. "We can change it."

Now I was a little worried. For the life of me, I couldn't figure out another room he would have had a reason to set up.

"Should I be terrified?" I asked.

"Possibly," he said with a laugh.

"Alrighty then." I grabbed his hand. "Let's go be terrified together."

∽

I WAS SPEECHLESS.

It was freaking heinous.

Gideon rocked back and forth on his feet nervously and watched me for a reaction. It took a Herculean effort not to laugh, groan or gasp in horror.

He'd decorated the nursery for our little girl… and then some. Although, *decorate* wasn't quite the correct word— more like he'd vomited up an explosion of pink lace. The walls were what I would have to call a Pepto Bismol pink and the carpet matched perfectly… so did the ceiling and all the trim. A massive pink crystal chandelier hung from above. It left an unfortunate rosy glow that eerily illuminated the scary pink room. And then there was the lace… There was so much lace, it was difficult to make out the furniture. Squinting my eyes, I spotted what I was fairly sure was the crib. It was a blush color with a canopy of shocking pink tulle trimmed in garish rose sequins. A pile of stuffed animals—all pink—were in a toybox covered in pale pink lace. The changing table was also sporting lace but stood out because of the glittery baby-pink fringe.

"Wow," I said, unable to find anything in my vocabulary more polite to say. At least I didn't scream. For a man with impeccable dress sense, his decorating skills sucked. It was shocking to reconcile that Gideon had created such a lovely house when I looked around the nursery. It would be seriously easy to lose a baby in this room.

"I might have gone a little far," he said with a wince.

Diplomatic. I needed to stay diplomatic. It would be plain mean to tell him it looked like a brothel for a baby. He'd clearly never seen a little girl's room before. "It's very lacy."

"Maybe a different shade of pink?" he asked, grimacing at the disaster he'd designed.

"Umm… no," I said, getting a slight headache from so much pink. "I love that you did this. I really do…"

"But?" he asked.

"But… I was kind of hoping we could do this room together," I said, glancing over at him with a smile. "No magic. I want to paint and go shopping for her stuff. I want to build her toybox and paint little animals and flowers all over it."

Gideon walked around the nursery and examined it. He shuddered. "It's fucking dreadful, isn't it?"

"Kind of." I laughed and wrapped my arms around him from behind. "But the thought counts for a lot."

"I got excited," he admitted, glancing around in horror. "I think my biggest mistake was talking to Candy Vargo."

My mouth dropped open. "Of all the people to go to for

advice…"

"I know. Pretty sure she punked me." He shook his head and grinned. "She said pink was the perfect color—told me to use it liberally."

"Well, you certainly followed directions," I said with a laugh. "Did she tell you to use lace?"

Gideon ran his hands through his hair and sighed. "No. That was my idea. Lace seemed girly."

"I see," I said, still grinning. "Maybe a little less would be better."

"Ya think?" he asked with a pained chuckle.

"Umm… yes. I say we scrap the lace."

"And I say I should electrocute Candy Vargo," Gideon added.

"Nope. You will not electrocute Candy Vargo because you went a little overboard."

"Little is a gracious description," he pointed out.

"I'm good like that." I was scared to see what he'd done to the master bedroom and hoped he hadn't chatted with Candy about that decor as well.

"So, you don't like lace?" Gideon inquired with a naughty smirk.

"In small amounts it's okay," I said, trying not to stick my foot in my mouth just in case he'd puked up lace in our bedroom too. I wanted to bang the man, not critique his interior design skills and make him feel bad.

"You're going to hate the master suite," he said, shaking his head.

"Oh my God. Seriously?" I asked before I could stop myself.

Gideon threw his head back and laughed. "Nope. I'm just playing with you."

I punched him in the arm. "You suck."

"Actually, I do," he replied, scooping me up and tossing me over his shoulder. "And I'm *very* good at it."

Hanging over his shoulder, I slapped his perfect butt. "I'll have to have evidence of that," I informed him as he slapped my bottom in retaliation. "I won't believe it until I experience it."

"Far be it from me to say no to my favorite person in the world," he said, snapping his fingers and making all the pink and lace disappear.

The room was now a blank slate, ready for both of us to create a haven for our baby. I was pretty sure after having experienced the pink baby brothel, I would avoid the color at all costs.

"That's the right answer, Reaper."

"Thought so, Angel," he replied. "Shall we take this to the bedroom?"

"Yep. I vote for getting busy immediately," I told him. "We have to get back to reality soon."

"This is reality," Gideon said, sliding me down his body and gazing into my eyes. "And reality is very, very good right now."

We never made it to the master bedroom. I had no clue if it was covered in lace and I didn't care. After the day we'd had, the four orgasms the Grim Reaper had given me made my world a much better and happier place.

He was indeed good at *sucking*.

And so was I.

CHAPTER FIVE

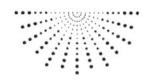

"I THOUGHT YOU ONLY FURNISHED TWO ROOMS IN THE house," I said, noticing something in the great room as we walked hand in hand down the stairs of our new home after a few very aerobic rounds of fabulous sex.

"You're correct," Gideon replied. "The master suite and Gideonia's nursery."

"Umm… that is *not* her name," I said with an eye roll and a groan.

"Just thought if I kept calling her that, you might cave and go for Mini-Daisy," he replied with a grin—then froze as we got to the bottom of the stairs. Gideon was no longer smiling.

Staring at the great room, I tried not to wince. It was as god-awful as the pink nursery but in a gothic way. The entire room was done in heavy, black wooden furniture with garish red accents. On top of an enormous black lacquered table sat an hourglass. Sparkling gold sand sifted through the thin opening between the globes and gave me an uncomfortable wonky feeling. Red velvet, floor-to-ceiling curtains hung from the windows and fluttered like a cascade of shimmering blood. Wrought iron torches, lit and mounted to the walls, cast an unholy glow in the large room.

"What the hell?" Gideon muttered, pushing me behind him and raising his hands in preparation to destroy whatever or whoever was here. "Show yourself."

Not a sound to be heard. Giving me a look, he gestured for me to stay where I was.

Not happening. If he was entering the hellish-looking room, I was going to be right beside him. I'd ended the life of an Immortal Angel less than twenty-four hours ago. If I could do that, I could handle a wannabe decorator with seriously crappy taste.

Gideon shot me an annoyed glance that I hadn't obeyed him, but let it go quick when I shot him a glance that beat his. I didn't fear the Reaper. I loved him. It was obvious no one had ever had his back. He was going to have to get used to it, or we would have problems.

"Do you think Candy Vargo did it as a surprise?" I whispered.

He shook his head. "No, it would have been filled with yard-sale buys if it was Candy. She's cheap."

That made sense. "Maybe my dad did it as a gift?"

Again, Gideon shook his head. "Not a chance—not his style."

The Grim Reaper's body was tense and his eyes blazed red. He waved his hands in a circular motion. An orchid-scented breeze danced through the room. I inched closer to Gideon and waited to see what would happen next.

His body relaxed somewhat, but his sharp gaze still roamed the room warily. "Whoever did this is gone."

"Can you tell who was here?"

"No," he said, slowly approaching the hourglass. "But my guess would be an Angel."

The answer was surprising. "I would have guessed a Demon due to the décor."

Gideon's eyes were glued to the sand in the hourglass. It was about two feet high and just as wide. The sand looked alive. "I do believe that was on purpose—probably a dig at me. However, no one but an Angel has access to the Celestial Dunes."

That was a new one for me, but lately my life was full of new information. My brain was having trouble keeping up. "The Celestial Dunes?"

He nodded curtly.

"Shut the front door. There are beaches in Heaven?" I asked, wanting to laugh.

"Not exactly," he said dryly. "Dunes. Massive piles of enchanted sand—or Angel dust, to be more accurate. I've never seen them—only heard talk. It's where an Angel goes to die. It's why the sand is so powerful."

"Angels die?" I asked, perplexed.

"Only by choice or by punishment," Gideon explained and pointed at the hourglass. "I can't touch it or I'll go up in flames."

"Can I?" I asked, grabbing his arm and pulling him back.

"I'm not sure," he admitted. "You're not a full Angel."

We were basically staring at a celestial bomb. Great. The violence in religious lore was astounding and stomach-churning.

"It has to be the assholes then," I guessed as I circled the table and examined the hourglass. "Maybe it's a warning from my delightful siblings about my tribunal for ending Clarissa."

"Possibly," Gideon ground out, staring daggers at the centerpiece. "I would so enjoy destroying them."

"Probably a bad plan," I said, wondering what we should do. "Daisy wants chocolate."

"What?" Gideon asked, glancing over at me in confusion.

"I said it was a bad plan," I repeated.

Gideon squinted. "Then you said you wanted chocolate."

"No, I didn't. I mean, chocolate sounds good, but I didn't say I wanted any."

"Actually, you did," he said. "Your exact words were, 'Daisy wants chocolate.'"

When the words were repeated, a little zing shot through me. I recalled saying them. What the heck? "I did say that, but I only remembered it when you repeated my words."

Gideon stared at me for a long moment. His expression was concerned. "Do you feel okay?"

Placing my hand on my forehead, I checked for a temperature. No temperature. I felt fine. I was tired, but it was going on two in the morning. I'd participated in an Immortal war of sorts in the morning, put June's soul back in her body then had some of the best sex of my life. To say it had been a busy day would be an understatement.

"I feel fine," I said. "Daisy can pick that up. We'll bring it back to the farmhouse. The others can help us figure it out."

Gideon narrowed his eyes. "We're not going to take that risk."

"What risk?" I asked, wondering if *he* was okay.

"Of you picking that up and taking it with us."

"That's a horrible idea," I said.

Gideon was now staring at me like I'd grown an extra head.

"What?" I asked.

"You just said you wanted to bring the hourglass to the farmhouse."

"No, I didn't," I said, then paused. Something new was happening. It was unnerving. I moved away from the hourglass just in case it had some kind of magically adverse effect on me. "Repeat exactly what you heard me say, please."

"You said, 'Daisy can pick that up. We'll bring it back to the farmhouse. The others can help us figure it out.'"

"Mother humper," I choked out, starting to shake. "Now I remember. Is the hourglass speaking through me?"

Gideon ran his hands through his hair and pressed his lips together. "I'm not sure. Whatever is happening, I don't like it."

"Do you think I'm lying?" I asked, confused and alarmed.

"Not following."

"The things I'm saying that I don't remember," I explained. "Do you think they're the truth?"

Gideon's chin dropped to his chest and he chuckled. "You're a terrible liar."

"Thank you," I said with an eye roll.

"Welcome. All of it sounded like the truth to me." He snapped his fingers and produced a chocolate bar.

"Ohhhh," I squealed, grabbing it and unwrapping it with speed. "Need this so bad."

The Grim Reaper watched with amusement as I made short work of the candy. "Well, the chocolate part was accurate."

"Yep," I said, licking my fingers. "Tell Daisy not to worry. She will be fine picking up the hourglass. She's the Angel of Mercy. The riddle must be solved before it's too late—many lives depend on it. *Time* is of the essence."

"Fuck," Gideon muttered.

I wrinkled my nose in embarrassment. "I know, licking my fingers is rude, but that was some really good chocolate."

"Not what I'm referring to," he replied. "Tell me if this rings a bell. 'Tell Daisy not to worry. She will be fine picking up the hourglass. She's the Angel of Mercy. The riddle must be solved before it's too late—many lives depend on it. *Time* is of the essence.'"

My knees buckled. Gideon moved with inhuman speed and caught me before my butt hit the floor. Burying my face in his chest, I tried to steady my breathing. "I remember. Who's talking through me?"

Gideon's arms tightened around me. His powerful magic bounced around the room, making it difficult to breathe.

"Tamp that back," I told him. "Too much."

He immediately reined it in.

I sucked in a huge gulp of air. "My gut tells me I'm telling the truth even though I don't remember saying it." I glanced over at the hourglass. "And the word *time* is important."

"I say we bring everyone here," Gideon suggested. "I don't want you touching that thing."

"What Daisy wants is more chocolate," I insisted. "However, *Gideon*... you are not the boss of Daisy. Yes, you are old. Yes, you are wise. Yes, you are powerful. But if you hold her back from who she is to become, you will lose her. Forever. And that is a very long time."

Gideon paled to the point I thought he was going to pass out.

Goddammit!" he roared. "Who are you? What do you want from Daisy?"

"What did I say?" My voice sounded wooden. I wasn't in control of myself and that could be very dangerous.

"You want it verbatim?" he asked, closing his eyes.

"I think that's the only way I can recognize it," I replied, wanting to cry.

He sighed and pulled me close. "You said, 'What Daisy wants is more chocolate. However, *Gideon*... you are not the boss of Daisy. Yes, you are old. Yes, you are wise. Yes, you are powerful. But if you hold her back from who she is to become, you will lose her. Forever. And that is a very long time.'"

"Well, that sucks." I pulled out of his embrace and walked right over to the table where the evil hourglass sat. "You need to shut your cakehole," I hissed at the sand inside the glass. "It's incredibly rude to spit your words out of my mouth. At the very least, you could let me hear them. You feel me?"

The hourglass didn't answer. I didn't expect it to.

"Whatever." I grabbed it before I could change my mind.

Gideon winced as I held the timepiece away from my body. It was lighter than I'd imagined it would be. I'd expected it to have a little heft, but it was as if the Angel-infused sand defied gravity. On top of that, the smooth, black marble spindles that held the hourglass in place were surprisingly warm...

"I'm not on fire. Right?" I asked, looking down at myself.

"Not on fire," Gideon said with so much relief in his voice, I laughed. "Let's move. The less time you have that damn hourglass in your hands the better."

"Fine by me," I said. "Transport?"

"Hell to the yes," he said, putting his hands on my shoulders and avoiding the magical time bomb in my hands studiously. "Ready?"

"Yes, I am. Get us out of here."

"As you wish."

CHAPTER SIX

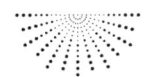

There was no need to call the group together. When we arrived on the front lawn of the farmhouse at 3AM, my home looked like a blazing beacon in the night. Every single light in the house was on. I spotted my father, Tim and a now older Candy Vargo through the bay window.

"And the story goes on," I muttered.

"The story always goes on," Gideon said. "We just need to control the narrative."

"The Angels are in there," I told him, glancing down at the hourglass in my hands. "I can feel them."

"Interesting. I don't sense them," Gideon said, surprised. "Shall we greet our *guests*?"

"Do we have a choice?"

"There are endless choices, Daisy," Gideon replied, raising a brow. "Some are better than others."

I laughed. It was either laugh or scream. The feeling of dread inside me was so extreme, if I screamed it could go on for hours. Laughing was the better *choice*. "Then yes. I vote we go in."

"Should we leave that outside?" Gideon asked, referring to the hourglass.

I shook my head. "Nope. My gut says to bring it in."

"You trust your gut?"

It was a legitimate question. Did I? I had little else to go on since the situation was so foreign. My gut had steered me wrong, but more often than not it had sent me in the right direction. "For the most part, yes," I told him.

"Good enough for me," Gideon replied.

"Really?" I asked, awed that he would put all of his trust in me… and a little terrified in case I was wrong.

"Really," he said, kissing my nose and keeping his body from coming into contact with the Angelic bomb. "Let's do this. If the voice speaking through you is to be believed, time is of the essence."

"That sucks," I muttered as I followed him across the yard and into my house. "And not the good kind of suck."

The minute we entered, all eyes shot to the hourglass in my hands. The already strained atmosphere grew stifling. Catching a break or a few hours without the threat of a deadly shitshow was impossible lately. Even my dogs were uncomfortable. They scooted their furry bodies under the couch with only their little snouts showing.

"Well, that's certainly a kick in the hairy clam," Candy announced, eyeing the hourglass warily.

"You're just foul," Heather said, giving her a disgusted glare.

"Thank you," Candy replied.

"Wasn't a compliment, idiot," Heather shot back, looking at the hourglass with cautious curiosity.

"It's Opposite Day," Candy said with a shrug and a raised middle finger. "This gesture means I love you."

"Put that finger back in your pocket or I'm gonna remove it," Gram warned Candy.

"Not if I shove it up her ass first," Heather muttered.

"Enough," Gideon snapped. "If you two have a go at each other, I'll be forced to electrocute both of you… and I'll enjoy it."

"Alrighty then," I said with an eye roll. "Let's ease up on the violent tendencies. I think I might have a little problem here. If you people feel the need to dismember each other, I'd suggest a truce or a rain check."

"I'd have to say *little problem* might be an understatement," Tim chimed in—literal as always.

"That right there is a colossal motherfuckin' problem," Candy added with a shudder, pointing at the hourglass.

Candy Vargo was no longer ten and she was no longer wearing sweatpants. In a few short hours, Gram had broken her. I was kind of shocked at how lovely she was. The Keeper of Fate was wearing lightweight woolen pants in a winter white with a matching cashmere sweater. Her hair was shiny and fell in reddish-brown waves down her back. I was pretty sure she was wearing a little makeup too. Gram was a miracle worker.

However, even though Candy Vargo's exterior was more refined, her vocabulary was not.

"Keep the Grim Reaper away from that shit," she advised, pulling a toothpick out of her pocket and putting it into her mouth. "He'll fry like a pig on a spit if he touches it."

"Already established," Gideon said, keeping his distance.

"What is it?" Missy asked. "I mean, I can see it's an hourglass, but I'm pretty sure it's a whole lot more."

"It is. It's basically a metaphorical time bomb," my father said flatly, staring at it with fury. "It was left for you?"

"That would be my guess," I said, placing it on the coffee table.

"No note? No directions?" he asked, his fists clenched at his sides.

"None," Gideon confirmed.

My mother's ghostly expression turned hard and angry. "Unacceptable. Daisy has been through enough already."

"Agreed," my father replied.

While I really wanted to get into particulars, it wasn't safe to do so yet.

Tim sat on the couch and took notes. Missy and Heather stood next to the fireplace. My mother floated in the air next to my father, who was standing at the end of the coffee table with his eyes fixed on the hourglass. Gram flew to my side and kept tabs on the new and somewhat improved Candy Vargo. Gideon stood in the foyer… away from the magical item that could set him on fire.

The Angels were nowhere to be seen, but that didn't fool me for a second.

"Charlie and June are still upstairs?" I asked.

"They are," Heather confirmed.

I looked at Tim. "Jennifer is safe at her home?"

"She is," he assured me. "Our friend is doing much better. Although—"

"Hold that thought," I said quickly. I knew we had invisible company. I didn't want them hearing anything about the possibility that Jennifer recalled what she'd witnessed. They'd already cast a spell on her to forget.

"As you wish," Tim said, a bit perplexed.

"And why is everyone here?" I inquired.

Tim held up his cell phone. "I received your text to come immediately."

"As did I," my father added.

"Yep," Candy chimed in. "You're gettin' a little fancy pants referring to yourself in third person."

"Crap," I muttered, running my hands through my hair and meeting Gideon's concerned gaze. "Was I on my phone after we discovered the hourglass?"

"You were not," he told me.

"Double crap. That doesn't bode well." The hourglass was apparently running my mouth right now… and my phone.

"Depends," Gideon said tightly. "Seems more friendly than deadly at this point."

I narrowed my eyes at the hourglass and watched the shimmering golden sand slip through the thin opening in the middle. The speed and amount seemed to vary with each passing second. It would be bizarre if it could actually see me, but I was ready to believe anything right now. The definition of impossible kept expanding.

"You want to explain what's going on?" my father asked. His eyes were glowing a blinding gold and his fury was barely checked. I was very aware it wasn't aimed at me, but he could be terrifying. The Archangel Michael was a deadly force of nature.

And he wasn't happy.

"I will. Later. I promise," I said, unsure that I could explain considering I was unclear myself. But most importantly, I didn't want the Angels to hear anything that could be used against me. I wasn't sure if anyone else was aware of their presence, but I was. They could play their game for a little longer. However, I planned to beat them at every turn. I had no clue if that was possible, but I'd try like my life depended on it… which it might.

My father nodded and accepted my answer without question. Maybe he felt them too. They were technically related to him, after all.

A chilly gust of wind blew through the living room. My dead squatters had joined the impromptu party. The Tasmanian Devil led the brigade. She looked ready to rumble or, rather, scare the shit out of someone. Five of them were here and they acted as if they'd just consumed a vat of espresso. That was impossible since the dead couldn't eat or drink. However, they seemed antsy and agitated.

"You will behave," I told the Tasmanian Devil. I pointed at her and she laughed. It sounded more like a death rattle than a laugh, but I understood dead people speak. It was part of my job and I was getting good at it. "I'm serious."

The Tasmanian Devil whipped down her ghostly pants and mooned me. The other ghosts cheered her on. It was like a deceased posse of second grade boys… except it wasn't.

"Duuuude," Missy said with a laugh that broke a little of the tension. "I do believe that departed derrière was aimed at you."

"I would have to agree," I replied, giving the Tasmanian Devil the stink eye as I tried not to laugh. "If your rear end falls off, don't expect me to glue it back on. You're on your own with that."

Gram cackled. "She's a spicy one. I like her."

I liked her too, but she was a menace. I was curious about her story, but I had too much going on to sit down with the nutbag right now.

"Was there any clue who left the hourglass?" my father asked.

Gideon looked to me. "Possibly."

"I think I might know who delivered it."

My father eyed me for a long moment. I winked at him. He raised a brow then winked right back. The Archangel Michael was quick on his feet. Or maybe our father-daughter bond was growing stronger. I'd put my money on both being true.

"I heard that Prue and Rafe are a *couple*," I announced, to the confusion of all but my dad and Gideon.

"Umm… that would be incest," Heather pointed out with a wince.

"Yep. Gross. But they are disgusting people," I pointed out in a loud voice.

The overhead lights blinked and a few pictures fell off the wall. Candy Vargo's smile grew wide. She understood immediately what I was doing. It made me a little uneasy, but nothing right now was calming. Having Candy join the fun could either be helpful or explosive. It was fifty-fifty. I was leaning toward volatile.

"Nah," she said. "I heard they like sheep. Especially Gabe."

Something in the kitchen blew up. I hoped it wasn't my coffee maker. It was the one appliance I couldn't live without.

Tim was right on Candy's heels of understanding the situation. The conversation was about to go south in a big way.

"Yes," he said, nodding enthusiastically. "From what I understand, Gabe and Rafe have many similar qualities to the proboscis monkey."

Heather laughed, fully on board with the game being played. "I'll bite. What do Rafe and Gabe have in common with monkeys?"

"Not just any monkey," Tim assured her with a naughty smirk. "The proboscis monkey specifically. When a male proboscis monkey is angry, he will jump up and down, shake branches and bare his teeth. However, he will also sprout a boner of pure rage. This boner will be displayed to his enemy as a warning. I like to refer to it as the wrath erection. Others call it the hatred hard-on."

That silenced everyone for a second. Tim was a loose cannon of horrifying information. It was fantastic.

The explosion in the yard was violent. I laughed. The Angels were not pleased. Screw them. "Do you have any illuminating facts about Prue and Abby?" I asked Tim.

"But of course," he replied. "Both Prue and Abby—like the ancient Egyptians—use crocodile feces as birth control."

"Umm… how?" Missy asked with a wince of horror.

"You do not want to know," Tim told her with a gag.

"Roger that," Missy said.

The lamp next to the couch went up in flames. Gideon waved his hand and doused it. "Is that all you got?" he asked the invisible guests.

It wasn't. The area rug beneath our feet disintegrated into slugs.

"Nasty," Heather said, snapping her fingers and restoring the carpet.

"Typical," Candy Vargo chimed in.

Before the Angels got more creative with the interior of my home, I decided the game had played itself out. "Show yourselves," I called out. "I know you're here."

As was their custom, they arrived with no fanfare. No wind and without a sound.

One by one they appeared. Rafe, Gabe, Abby and Prue might look angelic, but to me they were horrible people with weak morals and black hearts. They stood in a tight group under the archway between the kitchen and living room. All four had furious expressions on their attractive faces. Clearly, they were lacking a sense of humor, among other qualities that I liked in people.

I did not like them. Our shared DNA was irrelevant.

"I should incinerate all of you," Abby snarled. "That talk was blasphemy. We are to be revered."

"Reverence is earned," my father said in an icy tone.

"Isn't that rich coming from you?" Prue hissed.

"Well, you're just the little bundle of bitchy this evening," Heather said with a cool smile that came nowhere near reaching her eyes. "You shouldn't talk to your elders that way. It's rude."

"You're worthless," Abby sneered at Heather.

"Interesting coming from the lips of someone who would understand the word," Heather shot back.

"Truth hurts, don't it, assholes?" Candy inquired, pointing a toothpick at the foursome.

The Angels stepped back. Candy Vargo was not their favorite person. Again, I wondered what the hell she'd done to them. Again, I decided not to ask. My self-preservation instincts were growing daily. Plus, it would be embarrassing to puke right now.

Turning my full attention to the Angels, I glared at them. "You have some explaining to do," I said flatly.

"As if," Abby snapped. "I think you got that backwards. It is you who is under investigation."

"For performing your duty?" I inquired coldly. "For taking care of business? For picking up the ball that you dropped? For making you look like the lazy, careless Angels that you are?"

I could feel my eyes go gold. Everything in the room was glazed in a yellow haze. The shocked surprise on my siblings' faces didn't concern me. It was good to put a little fear of God—so to speak—into them. While they may have witnessed the deadly showdown between Clarissa and me, they didn't know the half of what I could do.

Actually, I didn't either, but that was for me to know and for them not to find out.

"Balls," Gabe commented in an amused tone. "She has rather large ones."

"Lady balls," I corrected him. "Far better than a rage boner."

He laughed. Maybe one of them could take a joke. I didn't have time to test if the others had a sense of humor and I really didn't care. I wanted them gone. Permanently.

"Why did you leave the hourglass?" I demanded, pointing at the coffee table where the offending object sat.

All four appeared dumbfounded. If I hadn't already experienced their deceitfulness firsthand, I might have believed they were as surprised as we were with the new nightmarish wrinkle. I didn't believe them. They were shits —lying, cheating, Immortal losers.

"Answer me," I ground out as they warily approached the hourglass.

Rafe squatted down and examined it with interest. Gabe scratched his head in confusion. Prue and Abby were strangely subdued. Not one of them touched it.

"I repeat," I said. "Why did you leave the hourglass?"

"We didn't," Gabe said, glancing around the room. "I've never seen it before—only heard tell of it."

"Same," Rafe agreed.

Prue and Abby were still mute and looked wildly uncomfortable. *Bingo*.

"I will ask once more politely," I let them know, staring daggers at the two women. "And you will answer me. If you choose not to, the repercussions will be hideous."

"Really fuckin' hideous," Candy Vargo announced with a delighted laugh. "More hideous than you could ever imagine, shitbags."

She looked over to Gram for approval.

"Good girl," Gram told her. "Don't think you needed the f-bomb, but other than that, it was strong and direct. Asshole might be a better choice than shitbag, but I'm not gonna fuss at you over that. Don't really wanna know what kind of heinous act you have in mind, but I'm dang proud of you for keepin' your middle finger to yourself. It's also real polite to give a warning before a smackdown as well. You done good, child."

Candy preened. The Angels appeared wildly perplexed how a ghost held sway over the Keeper of Fate. Whatever. It was good to keep them on their toes.

"I'm waiting," I said.

"We didn't do this," Prue said with no emotion in her voice except a touch of fear.

"I wish I could take credit," Abby said, sounding bored. "But sadly, I can't. Guess you're screwed, sister."

"Enough," my father bellowed as ominous sparks flew from his fingertips. "Lies shall not be tolerated. Damnation awaits those who deceive others of their kind."

The Angels had the smarts to cower away from the furious Archangel. They might be powerful, but my father—and theirs—was a badass of epic proportions.

"She's not a full Angel," Abby growled.

"I am," my father snarled. "Did you deliver the hourglass?"

They exchanged glances.

"No," Gabe said, meeting the Archangel's gaze. "We did not."

My father swore under his breath and gave them a look of utter disgust. "He speaks the truth."

"Okay," I said, remembering how literal they were. "They may not have delivered it, but do they know who did? Or why?"

"Answer my daughter," Michael said flatly. "Now."

It was brief, but I saw the pain pass over each of their faces when my father called me his daughter. It was hidden as quickly as it had appeared, but I witnessed it. As much as I despised them, a tiny part of my heart hurt for them.

Gabe inhaled slowly then shrugged. "No."

Not what I wanted to hear. But while we were playing the truth game...

"Who called the tribunal against me?" I asked. "Quite honestly, it seems redundant. Clarissa's crimes had sentenced her to death. Why does it matter who was the closer on the job? Not to mention it was self-defense for me and in protection of the Archangel Michael. The entire thing smells fishy to me."

Prue's swift intake of breath made me tingle all over—and not in a good way. Not one of them moved a muscle.

Unreal.

"Gram," I said tightly. "I'm asking forgiveness before I drop the f-bomb. Nothing else will suffice."

"Granted, baby girl," Gram said.

"Wait," Candy chimed in. "Will that work for me too?"

"Nope," Gram told her.

"Shit," Candy muttered. "Not seein' how that's fair."

"Life's not fair, is it?" I questioned aloud. "Abby, Prue, Rafe and Gabe know that. And when things don't go their way—or they don't uphold their end of the bargain, so to speak—they've learned to look for a workaround. You know… find a patsy to take the fall."

Heather growled and her enchanted tattoos began to dance on her skin. It was beautiful and frightening. "Shift the blame to cover their criminal offense."

"Find someone to pay the price for their own vile failure," Gideon ground out through clenched teeth as his eyes blazed red. "A distraction to hide their incompetence."

"It's your own fault. You should have waited until we arrived," Prue spat with condescending disgust. "As planned."

"Yeah, about that plan… It sucked. We would have been dead if we'd waited for you and your buddies," I said with an eye roll.

"Not our problem," Rafe said with a shrug.

"Clearly," my father said in a tone so cold it was scary. "Your lack of empathy is despicable."

Only Gabe had the grace to look remorseful. Maybe he was salvageable. Maybe not. Right now, not my problem.

"As the Arbitrator, I do believe this might be something I should look into," Heather stated. "Can't have assholes abusing the law. I'm quite sure the Enforcer will find the issue of interest as well. You might just end up regretting almost letting his wife die by your appalling disdain for an innocent human life—not very angelic of you."

"Blasphemy!" Abby shouted. "We are the law. Your blasphemous words are punishable by death."

"You certainly like the word *blasphemy*," I pointed out, going with my gut once again. "Tim, could you define blasphemy, please."

Not being very well educated in all things or anything religious, I crossed my fingers and hoped that I had the right meaning of the word blasphemy stored in my brain.

"With pleasure," he replied, clearing his throat. "Blasphemy—the act or offense of speaking sacrilegiously about God."

Win-win. My *gut* was on a roll.

I tilted my head to the side and smiled at Abby. Her eyes sparked dangerously. "Are you God?" I inquired casually.

Candy Vargo cackled. The Angels blanched. Gabe, Rafe and Prue glared at Abby.

"Are you?" I pressed.

They stayed silent. I'd expected them to. Abby had just damned herself.

"I thought not," I said as Gideon walked over and put his arm around me. I glanced up at him and he grinned. My confidence increased. "So, since you're not actually God, it seems to me that *you* are being blasphemous by throwing that word around in reference to yourself. Right?"

"Correct," Heather said. "Punishable by death… according to Abby."

"Abby, that's a real bummer," I said with a shrug, knowing there was no way I would have anything to do with harming her. I didn't like her. All I wanted was for her and her awful siblings to leave and call off the tribunal. She was a bitch, but bitchiness didn't equate with death in my book. However, she didn't have to know that. "Harsh punishment, dude."

The lights flickered and a sharp wind swept through the room, chilling me to the bone. The four Angels immediately dropped to their knees and my father bowed his head. The ghosts shrieked and disappeared. My mom and Gram followed them when my dad gave them a curt nod to leave the room. Gideon's arm around me tightened and he swore under his breath. My stomach dropped, and I felt like I'd just been busted for something huge. Could this twenty-four-hour stretch get any worse?

Apparently, yes. Yes, it could.

"And are you qualified to pass that judgment?" an unfamiliar voice inquired from behind me.

The sound and volume literally shook the foundation of my house.

"Fuck," Candy muttered, using the f-bomb I'd gotten permission to say and had neglected to use. "Let the shitshow begin."

I slowly turned and took in the intruder from head to toe. He was a walking, talking cliché straight out of the Bible. I almost laughed. Thankfully, I didn't. By the reaction of the Angels, I was pretty sure laughing wouldn't have ended well… for me.

An old man with flowing, pristine white robes and a beard down to his waist stood in the foyer. I'd guess him to be over six feet five, with sharp cheekbones and shrewd eyes. He was barefoot and his curly, snow-white hair gave his beard a run for the money. He held a staff in his hand made of glistening silver and a miniature horse sat on the floor next to him. A purplish-blue glow tinged with gold surrounded and illuminated him. His expression was bland. I couldn't tell if he was a friend or a foe.

Donna and Karen peeked out from underneath the

couch and growled. I heard a whoosh of movement behind me, but refused to take my eyes off the intruder. Was he God? Had he come down to take bloody vengeance on me? I was a little disappointed that God wasn't a woman. I should have figured it was a man.

"Daisy wants to know if your horse is potty trained," I informed him. "If he's not, you're gonna have to take him outside. Daisy's not in the mood for horse poop in her house. You feel me? And I like your beard. It's poofy."

The shocked gasps behind me alerted me that I'd spoken. I had no clue what I'd just said, but clearly, it wasn't good. The damned hourglass was going to get me killed.

"Are you serious?" the man demanded, wildly confused and insulted.

"Umm... not sure," I replied. "Gideon, can you help me out here?"

"Verbatim?" he asked.

"Unfortunately, yes," I replied as the man watched me with interest.

"You said, 'Daisy wants to know if your horse is potty trained,'" Gideon repeated. "Then you said 'If he's not, you're gonna have to take him outside. Daisy's not in the mood for horse poop in her house. You feel me? And I like your beard. It's poofy.'"

"Mmkay. Wow." I felt the heat rise from my chest and land squarely on my cheeks. "I'm usually a little more polite than that," I explained, thinking it might have been a bad idea to ask God to put his little horse outside and finish up by insulting his beard... but it *was* poofy. The hourglass was correct on that one. It felt like the hourglass had my back...

freaking bizarre. "But if you brought poop bags—you know, huge ones—or happen to have a horse diaper, that would be helpful… God… Sir… Your Almighty." My speech ended in a mortified whisper.

This wasn't going what I would call well.

The white-haired man threw his head back and laughed. He laughed so hard, I thought he might choke. It would be such bad form for God to die in my foyer. Was that even possible?

"My goodness gracious, I'm not God," he said, wiping the tears from his eyes.

"Who are you?" I asked, feeling like an incredible idiot.

"Unfortunately, right now, I'm your worst nightmare," he replied.

"How is this my freaking life?" I hissed. I was so done being threatened. His words set me off. I'd already dealt with my worst nightmare. This was bullshit to put it mildly.

Without thinking, I raised my hands and slashed them down through the air. A shimmering barrier dropped around Poofy Beard, trapping him inside. The Angels behind me gasped in horror. I was positive I'd just made a bad move, but I wasn't in the mood to die. I had a lot to live for.

The old man's eyes narrowed a bit and he chuckled. I wasn't sure if he was impressed or put out. He snapped his fingers and the barrier disintegrated.

Crap. If at first you don't succeed, try again.

With a grunt of frustration, I slashed my hands through the air again and imprisoned the intruder in an iron cage.

He clapped his hands and it completely disappeared. "This is fun. What else do you have up your sleeve?"

I had no clue how to answer. His guess would be as good as mine right now. If he wanted to be the guinea pig to test out my power, so be it. His idea of fun was warped.

In a flash, Gideon and my father transported. They landed right in front of me, shielding me from the unwelcome man.

Poofy Beard flicked his fingers and a blast of wind pushed them right back to where they'd been only seconds ago. It affected nothing in the room except the Grim Reaper and the Archangel.

Gideon swore profusely and my dad growled.

I was in way over my head and clearly on my own here.

"State your intention," I ground out, raising my hands yet again.

"Or what?" Poofy Beard shot back.

It was a fine question. "Or I don't know what," I shouted. "But I promise you it won't be *fun*."

The man shrugged. "Fair enough. I have not come to physically harm you. I've come to chat."

"You might have wanted to start with that," I pointed out. "Your social skills suck."

I was pretty sure I heard Candy Vargo snicker, but my body was filled with so much adrenaline, my ears were ringing.

"Please forgive my poor manners," the man said, sounding sincere. "I haven't been in the presence of those who breathe in quite a while. Shall we begin again?"

"Do I have a choice?"

He grinned. "Not really."

"You're not here to kill me or anyone else in my home?"

"Not today," he assured me.

My gut told me he was telling the truth. However, the truth where Immortals were concerned was a moving target. I didn't trust Poofy Beard, but I was going to have to trust my instincts.

"Fine," I said, somewhat ungraciously. While I didn't have as much power as the freak in my foyer, I did have more manners. I nodded jerkily and hoped that my coffee pot was still intact. When in doubt of being alive ten minutes from now, go back to ingrained habits. "Alrighty then, can I get you something to drink or eat?" My Southern roots ran deep.

The man's eyes grew wide with surprise. "That would be lovely, Daisy. I'll have a glass of water and some ambrosia if you happen to have any."

"Water? Yes. Ambrosia? No," I told him. "Would a banana work?"

He considered the substitution then nodded. "Fine. And a carrot for my pet if you can spare it."

The day had gone from violent to scary to wonderful to screwed up to weird.

And weird might just be the winner.

CHAPTER SEVEN

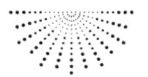

Strange and slightly menacing would be the most accurate way to describe the vibe in the living room after the man I'd mistaken for God had shown up. No one was at ease, but I didn't think a bloody Immortal battle was about to break out inside my house. There was no way Gideon or my father would be calm if Poofy Beard had lied and was going to attack me. I was a little torn about how to proceed since the man had announced he was my worst nightmare. Shockingly, he was very polite. It was difficult to reconcile the dichotomy.

"Zadkiel," my father said, eyeing him warily. "I was under the impression you were dead."

"So was I, shitbox," Candy muttered so softly I wasn't sure she'd even spoken.

I shot her a quick glance, but her eyes were glued to Poofy Beard, aka Zadkiel—whoever he might be. Again, my lack of religious knowledge was biting me in the butt.

The Angel laughed and fed his tiny horse the carrot I'd brought to him. When I got a better look at the animal, I wasn't sure it was a horse at all. I was certain it had growled. Horses didn't growl. The horse might be grumpy, but the man was incredibly jolly. If he had a big belly, I might have mistaken him for Santa Claus instead of God.

"Similar to Mark Twain, the rumors of my demise have been greatly exaggerated, Michael. I'm simply retired."

"Angels retire?" I asked, unable to stop myself. If he changed his mind and was here to eliminate me, I figured I had the right to ask some questions.

Zadkiel winked at me. "Only the wise ones."

Prue, Abby, Rafe and Gabe remained on their knees with their foreheads pressed to the hardwood floor. Zadkiel had given them a cursory glance then ignored them entirely. His focus was on me… and oddly, Gideon.

"So, it's indeed true?" Zadkiel inquired, his gaze bouncing with curiosity between Gideon and me.

"Is that why you're here?" Gideon asked, being cagey by answering a question with a question.

Immortals were both cryptic and vague from my experience with them. I wasn't sure how they got anything done. They were adept at non-answers.

Zadkiel shrugged and peeled his banana with meticulous care. "No. Just curious."

"Curiosity killed the cat," Gideon pointed out, staying by my side and refusing to answer the query.

I wondered if we'd broken some kind of celestial law by being together. Poofy Beard could shove it if he had an issue with us. I had Mini-Daisy Gideonia inside me. It wasn't in the plans for me to raise our horribly named daughter by myself. And I was sure both Gideon and my dad would have pointed out if our relationship was going to put us on Heaven's Most Wanted list.

Zadkiel nodded. "Alas, that is true, but cats have nine lives."

Tim cleared his throat and spoke up. He couldn't help himself. The Immortal Courier's knees bounced a mile a minute with excitement. When facts or myths were presented, he had to be in on the conversation. "According to an old English proverb: A cat has nine lives. For three he plays, for three he strays and for the final three he stays. Of course, nine is also considered a mystical number. Since cats have been both worshiped and feared through the ages for being magical, it all pulls together quite nicely."

Again, Zadkiel nodded. "They are also intelligent and intuitive. Cats have lightning-fast reflexes, quick decision-making skills and outstanding dexterity."

"If I may add a little something…" Tim said.

I was tempted to shout no, but I'd already been rude enough.

"Please do," Zadkiel insisted.

He was about to be very sorry.

Tim pulled a notebook from the pocket of his uniform and quickly found the page he was searching for. I held my breath.

"Ancient Egyptians—who used crocodile feces for birth control—also used to pluck their eyebrows off when their cats died. All family members would pluck their brows in mourning for their deceased felines."

Zadkiel's mouth formed a perfect O as he raised an unplucked, bushy brow. No one said a word. Tim was clueless that he'd just shocked the man. My buddy smiled with pride and tucked his notebook back into his pocket.

"Shave, asshole," Candy muttered with an eye roll. "Not pluck, shave."

"Interesting," Tim said, pulling the notebook back out and correcting his trivia. "Did you witness this during the ancient times?"

"Did it," Candy said. "Three times. Looked like an idiot. Took half a fuckin' year to grow my eyebrows back each time. I was pissed. Stopped having pet cats after that."

"Karma, I was wondering if you would speak to me."

"Well, fucker, I guess you got your answer. I was talkin' to mail boy, not you," she snapped, raising her middle finger, much to Zadkiel's delight.

What the heck?

"I must say, you are looking quite lovely," Zadkiel commented.

"And you're lookin' homeless, you shitbag," Candy Vargo shot back. "And fuckin' hairy."

Heather's eyes grew huge and Missy glanced down to hide her gasp. I was pretty sure Candy Vargo was about to bite it.

I was wrong… and seriously confused, as were Gideon, Tim and my dad, if their shocked expressions were anything to go by.

"Shall I change my appearance for your viewing pleasure?" Zadkiel inquired with an amused chuckle.

Candy narrowed her eyes then grinned. It was

frightening.

"If you can put your ass where your face is, it would work better for me, seein' as how all you do is spout shit out of your slimy piehole."

"Karma," my dad warned. "That is quite enough."

"Sure is," Candy announced, flipping Zadkiel off again. "I'll be in the urination station. If I have to smell ass, it may as well be my own."

And on that lovely parting shot, Candy Vargo left the living room. There was a story there, but I wasn't sure I wanted to know it. Ever. If Gram was in the room, Candy would have had her ass verbally chewed right off of her body. Her behavior was not exactly ladylike.

"Moving on. Shall we get to know each other?" Zadkiel asked me, ignoring the fact that he'd just been called some hideous names and flipped off twice.

If time was of the essence, we were wasting a whole bunch of it. I'd already been rude. I may as well continue.

"At the risk of being pushy," I said, thinking if Candy could get away with calling the Angel a shitbag, I could get away with making him get to the point of why he was here. "I'd like to know if you're responsible for the hourglass or here for the tribunal."

Zadkiel sighed dramatically. "Do we have to go there right now? I so rarely get to have fun."

Was the Angel right in the head? "Umm... yes. Time is of the essence."

His bushy brows arched and his little hairy horse-looking pet grunted. "Very well then. Do you know who I am?"

"You're Zadkiel."

"Not my name," he replied. "Do you know who I am?"

"Is that a trick question?" I asked, unsure of the rules. If I answered incorrectly, was I toast?

"No," he replied. "And by your answer it's quite clear you do not."

"That's not necessarily true," I said, buying time since I was pretty sure this was a test. I wasn't good at cheating, but I needed some help. It was getting close to sunrise and I was freaking exhausted.

"Gideon? Can you hear me?" I asked.

"Yes."

"Who is Poofy Beard?"

"Zadkiel's the Angel of Mercy," Gideon replied.

"Wait... I thought I was the Angel of Mercy."

"You are. Zadkiel is the original Angel of Mercy."

"So does that mean Poofy Beard is my boss?"

"It's not as literal or linear as that, but in a roundabout way you could say he's your supervisor. However, he's a deadly being and not to be trusted."

"He's a typical Angel then?" I asked.

"Nothing typical about the man. We all thought he was dead," Gideon replied. *"Listen to what he has to say. He tends to speak in riddles."*

"Immortals are a pain in the ass."

"Fine point. Well made."

"Are you finished?" Zadkiel inquired.

My eyes widened. I couldn't catch a break if I tried. "Umm... yes. Could you hear us?"

"Wouldn't you like to know," he replied, waving his hand

in a circular motion.

The poofy beard, the white robes and the long hair disappeared in a blinding flash of purple light. An enormous throne of sparkling silver now sat in my foyer with a very handsome and dangerous-looking man atop it. His sharp cheekbones and shrewd eyes were the same, but very little else.

"Much better," Zadkiel said. He was clad in black combat gear and armed to the point of ridiculousness. His blond hair was short and his demeanor seemed to match. His expression was unreadable, but it was clear he didn't suffer fools.

I wasn't a fool. I might not know what the hell was going on, but I was far from stupid.

"There's the son of a bitch I remember," Gideon said dryly. "The old man look was quite the show, Zadkiel."

The Angel shrugged. "Eternity is a long time, Reaper," he replied. "I enjoy switching it up. Keeps the boredom at bay."

"Does it?" my father asked, snapping his fingers and creating his own throne.

Where my couch had formerly lived, now sat a huge solid gold throne. It was far more ornate than Zadkiel's, but I was pretty sure that was the point of my father's gesture. Casually walking over to it, the Archangel Michael sat down and crossed his legs as if he hadn't a care in the world.

Shit was getting weirder.

"If we're playing that game, then I suppose I'll join," Gideon announced with a wave of his hand.

A shimmering black onyx throne appeared in a crack of blood-red lightning. The Grim Reaper's royal seating replaced my comfy overstuffed chair. I sure as heck hoped I'd get my furniture back after the male posturing was over. I liked my stuff.

Gideon grinned at his handiwork and sat down on his supersized throne.

I rolled my eyes. "What exactly are we compensating for here?" I asked, walking out of the front door and grabbing a rocking chair from the porch. I heard Heather and Missy laugh. Tim giggled. Plopping the rocker in the middle of the testosterone-fueled show of importance, I seated myself and rocked slowly back and forth.

"Are we all good now? Comfortable?" I asked. "Do all of you men have enough room for your egos and packages?"

"What did she say?" Zadkiel asked, shocked.

Gideon threw his head back and laughed. Even though I was a nervous wreck on the inside, the sound of his laughter kept me grounded. It was more potent than any magic I'd experienced so far. Weakness would get me nowhere fast. If Zadkiel had come for a showdown, I may as well go out on a high note with a few inappropriate jokes under my belt.

My father grinned. "Daisy made a most excellent point. And to answer the question, yes. Our egos and packages are very much at ease."

Zadkiel eyed me with interest. "So that was a joke you just made?"

I smiled and shrugged. "Nope. Not a joke."

"I see," he said, eyeing me. "Heather, Tim and Missy, you are excused. Daisy, Gideon, Michael and the four on the floor may stay."

My friends followed the request without question. It surprised me that he knew Missy's name, but I had a feeling he knew a lot. Heather gave me a loaded glance and led the trio upstairs. I was pretty sure she was going to talk to Charlie even if he and June were still working everything out. At this point, we all needed to be on the same page even though I wasn't quite sure what that meant. The fact that Zadkiel refused to call the Angels by name didn't seem to bode well, but that wasn't my problem… or I hoped it wasn't.

As the room cleared except for those deemed allowed to stay, Zadkiel's small horse hopped up and cuddled with the scary man. The animal was now sporting razor-sharp teeth and its eyes glowed red. Zadkiel had a Hell Hound just like me, or rather, I had a Hell Hound just like him.

Speaking of, Donna and Karen no longer had a couch to hide under since my dad had conjured up this throne. Donna zoned in on the animal on Zadkiel's lap and barked low in her throat. Very deliberately, she trotted over to where I sat and settled herself at my feet. Karen, clueless to the drama, wagged her tail and followed her furry sister's lead.

"Ahh, I see you have a Hell Hound," Zadkiel said, impressed. "Wherever did you find her?"

"At the pound," I replied, scratching Donna's head.

If Zadkiel was surprised, he refused to show it. Glancing over at the hourglass, I noticed that the golden sand had stopped moving. What did that mean? Was it good? Bad? Deadly? No biggie? My imagination was going to send me into a panic attack. Information was needed.

"Are you here for the tribunal?" I asked, ticking the first question off my mental list.

"There will be no tribunal," he announced, shooting the Angels a withering glance.

They couldn't see it due to their prone position, but I'd bet the secret recipe for Gram's chicken salad they could feel it. The Angel's displeasure bounced through the room like a deadly lead ball. Zadkiel was not messing around.

"Mmkay, good to know. Why did you bring me the hourglass?" I wasn't messing around either.

"And why do you think it was me?"

Holding back my eye roll took a lot of effort. If time was indeed of the essence, I wasn't in a position to lose any. The Angel could kill me where I sat with a flick of his fingers. Since that was the case, I had very little to lose. "Well, let's see… I destroyed Clarissa, was cornered into taking her job, put a soul back into a body that she'd stolen it from, then got ambushed by a magical time bomb. Coincidentally, you showed up and I just put two and two together. Of course, since you're the original Angel of Mercy, I figure you're here to test me or kill me. The *worst nightmare* thing wasn't exactly welcoming."

Zadkiel smiled. "It's all in the name. Study it."

"Study what? My name?" I asked, thinking maybe I should be taking notes.

The original Angel of Mercy wasn't nearly as polite as I'd thought. His eye roll was huge. "Not the way it works."

"Right," I shot back, topping his eye roll even though it was a risky move. "I forgot that being cryptic goes with the territory."

"Watch yourself," Zadkiel warned, his body tensing with displeasure.

He wasn't the only one displeased. All the words the Angel refused to speak had the potential to ruin my life. I felt it in my gut. Making him talk was my goal. The finish line was too far away right now no matter how fast I could run.

"Not sure that I have *time* to do that," I shot back. "Why is the hourglass speaking through me and why can't I hear what it says?"

The Angel appeared truly stymied for a moment. "It's not speaking through you."

I wanted to punch him in the head. "Lying is not becoming."

"Quite spicy," he commented.

I couldn't tell if that was a compliment or an insult.

Did it really matter? Nope.

"I prefer bold," I replied evenly. "So, are you going to explain the hourglass or are we going to play the guessing game, boss man?"

Gideon swore under his breath and quickly leaned forward, ready to pounce. My father jumped to his feet. It was clear I might have crossed the line. With no rules to the game, the parameters were invisible. I only had my gut. Slowly standing up, I gestured for my father to be seated and gave Gideon a look that let him know to back down.

Zadkiel simply smiled. Apparently, I passed.

"I've got this. He's here to test me." I stared at the man for clues. "I'll start. I have no idea what I'm doing or what I'm supposed to do."

"Obviously," Zadkiel said.

"Rude," I snapped. "I'm forty. And yes, I'm aware that in terms of years you have me beat by a long shot, but I'm old enough not to be embarrassed by admitting it when I don't understand. Not too long ago, I was a paralegal, nursing a broken heart. Now, I have dead squatters and more power than should be allowed. Pretending will get me killed. Already been pretty close to that and it sucked. So, here's the deal. You tell me what the test is and I'll take it."

"You think it's that simple?" he inquired, seemingly amused or possibly pissed.

It was a toss-up. I decided to go with amused with a small side of pissed.

"No, I don't. But the job I agreed to didn't exactly come with a handbook, so I'm winging it. Not sure how good I'll be at sending souls into the darkness since I'm the Death Counselor and I really like dead people, but I'll be fair. I can promise you that."

"Good to know," Zadkiel said, sounding bored. "However, that's the very least of my concerns. You have to earn your title or the price you pay will be higher than you could imagine."

"Alrighty then," I said, pressing the bridge of my nose. I could imagine some truly horrible things. "Is there a celestial website with job descriptions on it?"

"I don't even know what that means," he said, getting annoyed. "The handbook you seem so keen on finding is the Bible. It's a book of stories with morals. You should read it."

"On my to-do list," I said, refraining from adding it was one of the most violent books in existence. "However, I'm going out on a limb and guessing the hourglass is the key to how long I have to *earn* my place."

"Very good," Zadkiel said. "I shall call you Catherine."

"What?" I squinted at him and wondered if he had all his marbles. The non sequitur threw me.

"You're like a cat, hence Catherine—intelligent and intuitive. Cats have lightning-fast reflexes, quick decision-making skills and outstanding dexterity. We shall see if you can live up to the name. Daisy isn't a fitting Angel moniker," he informed me. "And if you die, I promise to shave my eyebrows in your honor."

He was nuts. Hanging on to myself was going to be important. I could only give away so much and still survive this crazy new world.

"No deal," I said flatly. "My name is Daisy Leigh Amara-Jones. I will answer to that—not Catherine."

"As you wish, but keep the name in your mind. You might need it," he said coldly. "The hourglass will empty itself in seventy-two hours. That is the time frame in which you have to prove yourself."

"To you?" I asked, wanting some sort of straight answer.

"To yourself… and me," he said flatly. "To be able to judge someone you must know what it is to forgive them. Judgment is a responsibility."

"That's it?" I asked.

Zadkiel paused for a long moment and stared at me. It was unnerving. "That's it. Find a way to forgive the ones who least deserve it—the ones who have taken the most. Sin is such a muddy concept. I find it thrilling."

I tried to wrap my mind around a mission that seemed far too easy. "How will I prove it?"

"Figure it out," Zadkiel said. "And I'd suggest keeping your friends close and your enemies even closer."

I nodded. My mind raced with questions that I was sure he wouldn't answer. The task was too simple, which probably meant it was as complicated as hell.

"And if I fail?" I pressed.

"Don't," he replied.

I blew out an audible breath of frustration. "Got that. But on the outside chance I do, is there only one chance to get it right?"

"There is only one chance to get it right," Zadkiel confirmed. "However, there are *endless* avenues to pursue to find the correct answers."

"Not really helpful," I muttered.

He smiled. "Not really trying to be. Where would the fun be if I held your hand and guided you?"

I rolled my eyes.

"Zadkiel, you are not permitted to assign a task without the consequences being stated," my father ground out, barely containing his ire.

"Says who?" Zadkiel demanded.

"Says me," came a terse and familiar voice from the stairwell.

Charlie walked into the room with his power on full display. It was a little difficult to breathe, but I didn't say a word—just took shallow breaths and hoped I didn't pass out. He looked exhausted and about thirty years younger than he had when I'd seen him earlier. He was a beautiful man. And he was a badass. His eyes shot silver sparks and his body literally glowed.

"Enforcer," Zadkiel said with a curt nod of respect. "Didn't realize you were here."

"Cut the bullshit," Charlie ground out, pulling back on his power. "Not buying it. State the repercussions if Daisy doesn't fulfill the task."

Zadkiel sighed dramatically and rolled his neck. The man was huge. "She loses time."

"More specific," Gideon demanded. "How much time?"

"Tedious people," Zadkiel muttered to himself. "The clock will go back to the day her husband died. Time will then resume, but it will end vastly different from the way it is now."

My mind swam with terror and my heart beat so loudly, I was sure everyone could hear it. The asshole wasn't just playing with my life, he was playing with the lives of everyone I loved. Most importantly, the bastard was playing with the life of my baby.

Not working for me. I didn't care who he was. Both of the Angels of Mercy that I'd met so far were despicable, horrid people.

"Are you serious?" I shouted, wanting to destroy Zadkiel just like I'd destroyed Clarissa. My hatred for Clarissa grew. She was the catalyst in so much pain and devastation. If I had the chance, I would end her again. "I'm pregnant. I know my father. I just got my mother back. Gideon is my reason... for everything. This is wrong."

Zadkiel scratched his Hell Hound's belly then shrugged. "Not my problem."

"Unacceptable," my father growled. "You have no right to pass such a judgment."

"Ahhh," Zadkiel said with a chuckle, ignoring the fact the Archangel Michael looked like he was about to blow. "That word again… *judgment*. Think about that, Daisy. That will be your savior or your downfall."

"Any other clues you care to share?" I ground out, hoping for something that made some sense.

"No, I'm good," Zadkiel announced then turned his attention to the four Angels still prostrate on the floor. "Your shoes are not ones I'd choose to walk in. The price for your crimes will be high—how high will depend on each of you."

Not one of them said a word.

Zadkiel turned and saluted us as if we were all friends. We were not, and I knew we never would be. "And the seventy-two hours begins… now."

In a burst of blue and purple crystals, the original Angel of Mercy disappeared with his throne and his Hell Hound. There was no trace whatsoever that the man had been here except one.

The hourglass.

And the golden sand was moving again.

"I would like to end that bastard," Gideon snarled. "And the four traitors on the floor."

Gabe, Rafe, Prue and Abby hadn't moved a muscle the entire time Zadkiel had been present. I was curious as to why, but cross-examining liars was not on the agenda… or maybe it was.

"Get up," I told them.

Slowly, all four rose and waited.

"I don't like you. I don't trust you," I said in a matter-of-fact tone. "However, you will be staying here."

"Wait. What?" my father asked, not liking the direction I was moving in.

"We're going to forgive them somehow, and they're going to forgive you," I said.

"Not a chance in hell," Abby snapped.

"Cakehole. Shut it," I snapped right back. "I'm going to take a stab in the dark and say the Angel of Mercy trumps *regular* Angels. Correct?"

The four exchanged furious glances.

"This is true," Rafe admitted grudgingly.

"Awesome," I said in my outdoor voice, feeling a little like I was about to lose my shit. "Then for the next seventy-two hours, I'm making the rules."

"And I'm breaking them," Prue announced with a vicious sneer.

Might wouldn't necessarily make right, but I was very aware that Angels understood violence and power.

"You sure about that?" I inquired.

"Positive," Prue hissed, and Abby laughed.

"Sorry," I told all four.

"For what?" Gabe asked, confused.

"For this," I said, slicing my hands through the air and putting them in an iron cage filled with spikes that trapped their hands at their sides. I didn't need them casting spells. "Can they break out of that or cause us any trouble from inside?" I asked Gideon.

Gideon snapped his fingers and the cage began to glow

and hiss. "No. They can't."

The expressions on their faces would have been amusing if I wasn't about to fall asleep on my feet.

"You will *not* get away with this," Prue growled.

"Already did," I said then turned my back on her. "Charlie, is June okay?"

"Getting there," he replied, glancing around the room. "Is there a reason you've redecorated with thrones?"

I laughed. "You're going to have to check in with the egos and the packages on that one," I told him. "I need to sleep for a few hours. I know I'm wasting precious time, but I'll waste more if I can't think straight."

"Sleep," Gideon insisted, gently pushing me toward the stairs. "We will watch over your new roommates."

"As long as *watch* isn't a euphemism for electrocute, I'm good with that."

Gideon grinned. "Damn, busted. However, for you, I shall refrain from my natural tendencies where lowlife Angels are concerned."

"Thank you," I said with a tired laugh. "That's very kind of you."

I took the stairs one at a time. My new roomies bitched loudly about the turn of events, but I didn't care. They could complain all they wanted to. The enormity of what I could lose was too overwhelming to think about. So, I didn't.

I'd sleep for three hours. That would give me *sixty-nine* hours to save my world. I giggled at the number sixty-nine like a middle-schooler. Right now, I'd take a laugh wherever I could find one.

Shit was about to get real.

CHAPTER EIGHT

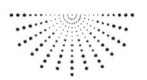

"Waaaaakahuuuuupha!" a voice bellowed into my ear. "Tiiiiimah tooa maaaakha theeeee doooounuuuts!"

Jackknifing to a sitting position, I screamed. For a second, I had no clue where I was or what day it was, but I was positive I was late for something. Bright morning sunlight streamed through the windows and I was tangled in the cozy flannel sheets. "What the hell?" I shouted, spying the individual who thought taking a few years off of my life was a good idea.

I was home in my bed. A directionless mission lay in front of me with horrifying consequences if I failed. And a naughty ghost had decided to scare the bejesus out of me. Awesome.

The Tasmanian Devil was thrilled with herself. I was not. Glancing over at the clock on the bedside table, I sighed. According to my plan, I only had five more minutes of my allotted three hours to sleep. While I wasn't happy to lose the extra minutes, at least the dummy hadn't messed up my schedule too badly.

"Is there a reason you're such a pain in the ass?" I got out of bed and pulled on some yoga pants and a soft, thick, green cotton sweater. Since I had no clue what I was going to be doing in the next sixty-nine hours, I figured I should be comfortable.

"Doooounuuuts," she repeated, zipping around my bedroom.

"You can't eat," I reminded her, shaking my head. "You're dead."

She cackled and turned backflips. "Waaaaakahuuuuupha!"

"I am awake," I said with a tired laugh. "You succeeded."

"Ssssoooorrry, Dausseeeeee." She tried to look contrite. She failed miserably.

"Nope. You're not sorry," I told her, putting on my favorite tennis shoes.

"Naawwwooo, nooooota ssssoooorrry," she agreed, sitting down on the floor next to me.

I stared at her and she stared right back. For a brief second, I saw such sadness in her sunken eyes, it took my breath. What had happened to the Tasmanian Devil in life? If I had to guess her age, I'd put it close to my own. She looked to be somewhere in her forties—possibly later forties. She was missing part of her jaw and her head was a little misshapen, but I found her pretty in a bizarre way. Initially, I'd been appalled by the appearances of the dead, but I'd learned quickly how deceiving looks could be.

Beauty was in the eye of the beholder. My deceased squatters were all beautiful to me in their own way.

"Soooooooftah. Preeeetah," she said, admiring my sweater.

"Thank you." I extended my arm so she could feel it. Her hand went right through the material and I felt her cool fingers on my arm. Sometimes the ghosts were more corporeal and sometimes more transparent. Each entity was different and special.

Her body was in decent shape as far as being dead was concerned, aside from her partial missing jaw. It made me think she hadn't died all that long ago. The amount of decay was a clue as to how long my deceased guests had been hanging around. I never pushed anyone to leave. I waited until they came to me and were ready for my assistance to fix what they needed help with before they could move on.

I had a feeling the Tasmanian Devil might be ready. Problem was, I didn't exactly have the time right now.

"Dausseeeeee," she said, pointing at me.

"Yep?" I asked.

"Tiiiimah."

Time. The word kept popping up lately. It made my stomach roil.

"Time for what?"

Yoooooah," she replied. "Meeeeeeah."

I glanced down at the floor. The floral rug wove an intricate pattern. The vines and flowers never seemed to start or stop, they just kept going—no end in sight. My life was my carpet or at least I needed it to be. The end could not be near. Believing I would fail was stupid and counterproductive.

"What's your name?" I asked.

"Taaaaaarrrah." She extended her hand to me.

I took it in mine and giggled. Feeling the touch of a ghost was a gift that came with being the Death Counselor. "Tara is perfect," I told her with a grin. "It sounds enough like *terror* to fit you."

"Yausssss," she said gleefully. "Taaaaaarrrah theeeeee teeeerrrrorah!"

"You got it." I stood up and considered my options. There were about a thousand. The Angels were caged in my living room, June was somewhere in my house, Tara the terror wanted to talk—which meant mind diving—and Zadkiel the jackass had suggested I read the bible.

Where in the hell did I start?

"Coffee," I said. "I need iced coffee with a huge squirt of chocolate syrup. You in?"

Tara nodded and shot herself up to the ceiling like a bullet out of a gun. If she'd been alive, she would have knocked her head right off of her body on impact. She was dead. If her head fell off, I could superglue it right back on. I'd already repaired a few noggins in my short time as the Death Counselor.

"I'm on double duty—Death Counselor and Angel of Mercy," I told my crazy buddy. "And I promise you we'll talk. I'm kind of in a crunch right now with less than sixty-nine hours to figure something out… or else my world falls apart."

The words sank in hard as I said them. I took a deep

breath to stave off a panic attack. There was so much to do, I felt paralyzed. Main problem was, I didn't know where to start.

"Whhhhaaaza proooblemah?" Tara asked, floating back to me and touching my cheek gently.

The question was so odd, I laughed. The sound was thin and tinny, but laughing was a relief. Tara the terror had it backwards, but the sentiment was sweet. Her touch was comforting. I was supposed to help my ghosts, not the other way around. But… desperate times called for unusual measures.

"I hate to burden you," I told her hesitantly.

"Naawwwooo prooobleemah," she insisted. "Taaaaaarrrah ahh nuuuunah. Looovah heellpah."

"What?" I asked, shocked.

"Whaaat?" Tara repeated as if we were playing a silly game.

"What did you just say you were?" I was sure I'd heard her wrong.

"Taaaaaarrrah ahh nuuuunah," she said again.

"I'm so sorry," I choked out, trying my best not to laugh. I was not successful. "You were a *nun*?"

"Yausssss!" she said, making the sign of the cross.

It was a little difficult to reconcile that the ghost I'd been mooned by earlier had been a nun in life.

I squinted at her. "Is that the truth?"

"Ohhhhh, yausssss," she said. "Nuuuunah."

I was still having trouble wrapping my mind around the new information. Tara was nothing like what I imagined a nun to be. Nuns were supposed to be somber and holy…

and carry rulers to smack hands with. I grinned. I had no clue what I was talking about. Religion was like Greek to me and I didn't speak Greek. Maybe all nuns mooned people. I doubted it, but…

"Have you read the bible?" I asked, feeling a little tingle shoot through me.

Maybe… just maybe things were happening for a reason right now. Or else I was nuts. Well, I *was* nuts. But it was either accept the crazy or go crazy. I decided to welcome it.

Tara zipped around the room like a balloon with the air coming out of it. "Yaussssss! Biiiballl ssschooolarah."

"Shut the front door," I said with a laugh. "Do you have time for some quick Sunday School lessons for me? Like a CliffsNotes version of the Bible?"

"Yausssss, Dausseeeeee," she replied, diving into my sock drawer and coming out of my underwear drawer.

She was a hot mess and incredibly active, but she'd grown on me like a non-poisonous rash that only itched occasionally. I liked the nutball with the semi-psychotic need to scare the shit out of everyone. I'd never heard of a nun called Tara, but then again, I didn't know many nuns—or any nuns. From a documentary I'd watched at least a decade ago, I kind of remembered nuns being given different names when they signed up or whatever they called it.

"Is Tara the terror your given name or your nun name?" I asked, walking into the bathroom to pee and brush my teeth.

"Ohhhhhhhh," Tara squealed with joy as she entered my bathroom.

The bathroom was off limits to the ghosts, as well as my bedroom. Sister Tara was a Heavenly rulebreaker.

I shook my head and laughed. "Yep, don't get used to being in here," I warned her. "I have to have a few places that are just mine. You feel me?"

"Yausssss," she answered. "Biiiirrrth naaaamea Taaaaaarrrah. Sisssssstah naaaamea Caaatheerinee."

I almost choked on my toothbrush.

"Catherine?" I whispered with a mouthful of toothpaste.

Zadkiel's words echoed like a bomb in my mind— *Catherine—intelligent and intuitive. Cats have lightning-fast reflexes, quick decision-making skills and outstanding dexterity. Keep the name in your mind. You might need it.*

"Sisssssstah Caaatheerinee," she confirmed.

An out-of-body sensation consumed me and I felt like I was watching myself from above. Had the asshole Angel helped me? On purpose? Had he given me clues that would actually help?

I was going to go with a yes. Sister Catherine was now going to be my wing-woman. It might be a disastrous mistake, but with very little to go on it was the best I could do.

"I need you," I said, extending my hand to her.

"Yausssss, yooouah dooooooaha."

I had a Ouija board. I could use it to speak with her, but mind diving was my best bet. It would have to wait a bit. I needed to check on what the heck was happening downstairs. Pronto.

"Sister Catherine, you ready for an adventure?" I asked,

splashing cold water on my face and quickly twisting my wild curls into a messy bun.

My new ghostly *nun* buddy whipped down her pants and mooned me. It was a wildly unholy move, but it was definitely funny. I took her transparent bare bottom as a yes.

"Reeeaaady?" she asked, quivering with excitement.

"No, but that's irrelevant. Ready or not, here we come."

∼

"Where's the cage?" I asked, worried that the Angels had escaped and left. That would suck for so many reasons. Forging—or rather forcing—forgiveness with them and my father was the only thing I could think of as far as succeeding at my life-altering task. If they were on the loose, that would make it very difficult. Plus, they were not nice people. I didn't need to deal with them trying to exact payback from me. It wasn't on my tight schedule.

"In the laundry room," Heather told me with a wicked grin. "The inhabitants were getting noisy and seriously rude."

"The laundry room is kind of small," I said, pulling on a few tendrils of hair that had escaped my bun.

"I shrunk the cage a little," Heather said. "They were thrilled."

I could only imagine. The longer I left them imprisoned, the meaner they would get. Letting them out was risky. "Keeping them here might be a bad move."

"No move is a bad move right now," Missy pointed out. "Not moving is the only thing that would be bad."

I nodded and peeked over at the hourglass on the coffee table. The golden sand streamed through the opening. It was noiseless, but I could hear the imaginary ticking time bomb echoing loudly in my head.

Move. Keep moving. Deal with the now then each second after.

"Is my furniture gone for good?" I asked with a frown, glancing around my noticeably bare living room. At least the thrones were gone.

Gideon looked sheepish as he handed me my favorite caffeinated morning drink. "I couldn't recall exactly what the furniture looked like."

Taking a healthy sip and walking over to the side table that had somehow survived being displaced by the thrones, I opened the drawer and pulled out a photo album. Pushing down a rush of sadness I could feel coming on, I found a picture of me and Steve in our furnished living room. It was a terrific picture of us, and the couch and chair were in full view.

Gideon peeked over my shoulder then put his arms around me. "As the Angel of Mercy, you can see him again," he whispered. "Once."

The news was shocking, wonderful and strange. "I can?"

He nodded. "You can. But I would suggest saving it."

I was too overcome to speak. Seeing Steve again would be magical, but I had to prove myself to even keep the job of Angel of Mercy... and I would. I had to. Too much was at stake.

Gideon studied the picture of the living room then waved his hand and restored it to its comfortable glory.

"I feel panicky. I'm not sure what to do first. Actually, I'm not sure what to do at all," I told him as I rested my head against his chest then changed my mind and began to pace.

He was quiet for a moment as he considered what I'd said. When he spoke, his voice was even and sure. "Go about your business as usual. Deal with what's right in front of you. Answers have a habit of revealing themselves when they're supposed to."

His words felt right. They calmed the tsunami developing inside me. "How'd you get so smart?"

"I'm old."

I smiled. "Understatement."

"Daisy?"

I whipped my head in the direction of the voice. June stood in the archway dividing the kitchen and living room. She was wearing the clothes I'd left for her and she still appeared to be twenty-five years old. The strangeness of it made me uneasy, but the alternative would have been devastating.

"June," I said, crossing the room and wrapping my arms around her.

I missed her plumpness. Hugging her felt wonderful, but kind of wrong. What had she lost in the transition besides a few pounds and a lot of years? She clearly remembered me, but did she recall her entire life?

"I'd like to talk," she said softly, holding on to me like I was a lifejacket and she was drowning.

"You got it." I hugged her tighter. I couldn't even imagine

what she was feeling. Actually, maybe I could. A few short months ago, I'd known nothing of the Immortal world around us. I still felt like I'd only cracked the tip of the iceberg, but I wasn't afraid of it anymore. "Alone?"

She gave Heather, Missy and Gideon an apologetic smile. It was classic June. She hated hurting people's feelings. "If that's okay, yes."

"More than okay," Heather assured her with a warm smile.

"Absolutely," Missy concurred. "Heather and I need to go home and shower and change clothes. We'll be back in an hour."

"Where are my mom and dad?"

"Went home to sleep, and I would guess, plot," Missy said, straightening the pillows on the couch. "They'll be back soon."

"We can talk later," June said, squeezing my hand.

"No," I told her. "Just give me a few to get my head straight."

I wrung my hands. I wanted to run for miles and miles. Icy wind on my face might clear my mind. Nothing was happening that would help me prove to myself or Zadkiel that I deserved to be the Angel of Mercy. Hell, I didn't want to be the Angel of Mercy. I just wanted to be the Death Counselor.

Oh my God. Wait. I had to *want* to be the Angel of Mercy. I associated the title with Clarissa. I despised Clarissa with every fiber of my being. Even thinking about her was infuriating. A small part of me was terrified I'd become like her since I took the job. Ridiculous? I hoped so.

I was nothing like the horrid excuse of an Angel. As long as I stayed grounded and remembered what was important, I could hold on to myself. I had to.

It was time for an attitude adjustment or a valiant attempt.

"Business as usual," Gideon reminded me.

I took a deep breath and expelled it slowly. "I'm the Death Counselor."

No one said a word. I'd confused them.

"I'm the Angel of Mercy."

June patted my back lovingly. "Are you having an identity crisis, dear?"

"Yep," I confirmed with a slightly inappropriate laugh. "That's a given. I'm working on overcoming it."

"You're doing just fine, sweetie," June assured me. She might look twenty-five, but she was all June.

"I'm the soon-to-be mother of Mini-Daisy Gideonia."

"Oh my hell," Heather choked out on a laugh. "That's her name?

"It's a placeholder," I said with a wince.

"Thank God," Missy said.

"Damn fine fuckin' name," a very recognizable voice shouted from somewhere in the house.

I glanced around and looked for the owner. "Where's Candy Vargo?"

"In the *urination station*," Heather replied with a shake of her head. "She hasn't come out since she went in there."

"What's the deal with her and Zadkiel?" I asked.

"Not a clue," Heather admitted. "Last night was the first time I'd ever been in his presence."

I glanced at Gideon, who shrugged. "I have no idea and can assure you that I'd like to keep it that way."

"Roger that." It was probably best to leave some things a mystery. The thought of Zadkiel and Candy Vargo together was one of those things. "Has anyone tried to get her out?" I asked, wondering if she was okay.

"Yep, I tried," Gram said, floating into the living room. "She won't budge. Just sittin' in there on the closed commode pickin' her dang teeth. Got me worried. Tim's in there tryin' to bribe her to come on out. That boy even volunteered to let her decapitate him."

"The weird just keeps getting weirder," I muttered.

"You can say that again," June said with a giggle.

The sound of her giggle was music to my ears. As freaked out as she had to be, she could still find joy. That was part of the key to staying true to myself. I needed to keep finding the joy. And speaking of joy in a roundabout, butt-baring kind of way…

"I want to introduce you guys to someone who I think can help," I said, looking around for Sister Catherine.

As if on cue, Candy Vargo and Tim screamed bloody murder and tripped over each other as they tried to escape the guest bathroom. Sister Catherine was right behind them, howling like she was on fire. The crazy ghost was taking her job as my wing-woman seriously.

"That damned see-through cadaver is a menace," Candy grunted, flipping Sister Catherine off.

Sister Catherine went to her signature move and mooned the Keeper of Fate.

"The Tasmanian Devil is a nun," I announced. "Her name

is Sister Catherine."

There was a moment of perplexed and shocked silence. I didn't blame them. It was a lot to swallow considering her behavior.

"Seriously?" Tim asked, reaching into his pocket.

Candy rolled her eyes and laughed. "Of course she's a dang nun. What did the nun say at the salad bar?"

"Whaaaaaaatah?" Sister Catherine asked, flying in circles around Candy

"Lettuce pray," Candy said as the nutty nun cackled with delight.

"Whaaaaatah doooo youuah callllllll aaah slleeepahwall-lllkiin nuuuunah?"

"Are we really sharing nun jokes?" Gideon asked, bewildered.

I grinned. "Apparently."

"Fine," he said with a chuckle. "A sleepwalking nun is a roamin' Catholic."

"Yausssss!" she squealed. "Mooooorah!"

Tim raised his hand politely. "May I, Sister?"

"Yausssss!"

"I once met a nun who wiped her nose on her clothing… she had a nasty habit," Tim announced with gusto, reading from his ever-present notebook.

I quickly glanced over at Sister Catherine to gauge her response. She bellowed with laughter. It sounded like she was choking to death. Since she was already dead, I didn't worry. And it figured she would like Tim's off-color pun. She was into mooning people.

"What do you call a nun's bowel movement?" Candy

Vargo shouted.

Karma was all in.

Heather winced. "That might be pushing it."

"Nah," Candy said. "Sister Scare the Shit Out of You has a sense of humor. Right, Penguin?"

"Riiiiightah, jaaackahassssss!"

Candy's mouth fell open. "Did the penguin just call me a jackass?"

"She did," Missy said with a laugh.

"She nailed it," Heather added.

Candy flipped Heather off then eyed the flying religious specter.

"A nun's BM is called holy shit," Gabe called out from the laundry room.

I closed my eyes. The conversation had veered into the absurd. The Angels were now involved. How was this my life?

Sister Catherine rolled around on the floor and laughed so hard her left arm fell off. Sighing and walking to the kitchen, I grabbed a tube of superglue. I was staying in the moment. I didn't need a wing-woman with a missing arm.

"You going to let us out of here?" Abby grumbled, hearing me in the kitchen.

"Are you going to behave?"

There was silence. I had to give it to them. At least they didn't lie.

"I'll figure it out after I glue the nun back together," I called out.

And I would. There was no choice because time waited for no one and I didn't have much of it left.

CHAPTER NINE

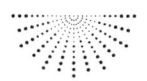

"Did you say *weed nuns*?" Prue asked Tim, wrinkling her nose in disbelief while sitting on the couch with her sister and brothers.

They looked wary and uncomfortable, but they were doing their best to fit in and not get electrocuted by the Grim Reaper—who was itching to set them ablaze. Prue and Abby had even conjured themselves up some yoga pants, tennis shoes and sweaters, thinking that was the uniform. I held my tongue and was thankful the men weren't wearing yoga pants as well. Truthfully, I felt sorry for them, but I reminded myself that they could have cared less if I was dead. Their absence at the showdown with Clarissa spoke ugly volumes that were hard to deny.

After a lengthy negotiation where Gideon had threatened an electrocution that would leave the four Angels without four of their five senses for an eon, they grudgingly agreed to behave. Mentioning Zadkiel's displeasure with them helped as well. The retired and obnoxiously cryptic Angel of Mercy struck fear in my siblings.

I was concerned that our definitions of *behave* might vary, but time was of the essence. Forgiveness was going to be hard to achieve if they were locked in a cage. They were my best bet so far since they were the ones least deserving of forgiveness. As soon as my dad came back, we'd give it a shot.

The Grim Reaper had warned he would take their sight, hearing, and ability to taste and smell. He would graciously leave them with the sense of touch so they could experience the pain that he promised he would happily administer daily for the next couple of centuries. The entire conversation was violent. However, it worked. Angels and Demons were interesting breeds.

"I did say weed nuns," Tim replied, nodding in excitement.

"Pot penguins," Candy announced, sitting next to Sister Catherine on the overstuffed chair.

The two had bonded after Candy mooned the ghost and offered to share her toothpicks. The nun couldn't actually use a toothpick since she was dead, but clearly appreciated the gesture. They made a motley pair, but both seemed pleased by the new friendship.

Gram was thrilled Candy had made a buddy even if she was a ghost. Gram had spent a good half hour trying to explain how baring your ass in public wasn't ladylike. Neither woman seemed to grasp the idea... or care. My understanding of nuns was getting a workout. Although, I suspected Sister Catherine might be an outlier as far as holy women went.

The Angels, while behaving, kept a healthy distance from Candy Vargo. Every time Candy spoke, they paled. An idea occurred to me, and I tucked it into the back of my mind for later. One thing at a time. Zadkiel had said there were *endless* avenues to pursue to find the correct answers. Not really helpful, but I was making a list of side roads just in case the main avenues were filled with traffic.

"In Northern California, a sisterhood grows cannabis," Tim said. "The sisters take vows, live together, work and pray with each other, but are not affiliated with any specific religious sect."

"Heard of them," Candy said. "Those penguins crank out Mary Jane and sell it."

"Yes and no," Tim explained. "It's actually hemp, which means it's not for getting high, more for the healing properties of CBD. The money earned goes to charitable causes."

"Betcha they indulge," Candy said with a laugh.

"Yausssss," Sister Catherine shrieked, whipping down her trousers in agreement.

The Angels weren't sure what to do with that. Honestly, I wasn't either. And I needed to talk to June.

"Gideon, can you referee without setting anyone on fire?" I asked as I stood up and nodded to June to follow me. Never in my life did I think I'd ask a question like that and be serious. The times, they were a-changin'.

"Depends," he replied, glancing at Prue, Abby, Rafe and Gabe. "It's up to them."

"We shall behave," Prue hissed rudely.

Abby rolled her eyes in annoyance. Rafe was blank-faced and emotionless. Gabe was the only one with a hint of a smile on his handsome face. I wanted to like him, but something held me back. The fact that they'd left me and my father to be killed by Clarissa might have a little something to do with it.

"And I will make sure they do as well," Charlie said, entering the room. His hair was wet from a shower and he was wearing some of Gideon's clothes. The Immortal Enforcer looked the same age as June. They were a handsome couple. He kissed June and ran his hand lovingly over her cheek. "Trust me," he continued, looking over at the Angels with a scowl that sent shudders skittering up my spine. "They *will* behave. Gideon's consequences will look like love pats compared to what I will do."

I wasn't sure that completely emasculating the Angels was the best plan, but they'd left me with little choice. As my father—and theirs—had told them, *reverence had to be earned*. Trust did as well.

"Charlie," June chastised her husband with pursed lips. "You'll catch more bees with honey than vinegar. You be nice to those poor people."

Gabe cleared his throat. "June… may I call you June?"

"Certainly," June said with a smile as Charlie glowered menacingly at Gabe.

"To be fair, the Enforcer has every right to be vengeful," he said.

Prue, Abby and Rafe glared at him like he'd lost his mind.

"You do *not* speak for us," Rafe said, waving his hand dismissively at Gabe.

"Weak," Abby snarled.

"Shut up, Gabriel," Prue hissed.

"Why, Pravuil?" Gabe demanded, narrowing his eyes at her in fury. "You heard Zadkiel. Our shoes are not ones he wants to walk in. The price for our crimes will be high—how high will depend on each of us. He basically laid out our death sentence. If you want to go to your maker with blood on your hands, so be it. I have a few days to make some of it right. So, fuck you if you don't like it."

My eyes widened. Nuns mooned people and Angels dropped f-bombs.

"I think that's a lovely idea minus the colorful language, Gabe," June said.

"Amen," Gram hooted.

June didn't acknowledge Gram. I wasn't sure if she knew Gram was with us. However, she was staring at the Angels with a strange expression on her face.

"What?" I asked, worried.

June shook her head absently and smiled. It was an odd smile. "Let's go talk, Daisy. Please."

∼

"I REMEMBER," SHE WHISPERED AS I CLOSED AND LOCKED THE door to my bedroom.

A lock wouldn't keep anyone out, but it felt definitive. At the very least, someone would think twice about interrupting. Well, not Sister Catherine, but she was busy being BFFs with Candy Vargo.

"You remember your life?" I asked, looking around my messy bedroom in embarrassment. Cleaning wasn't high on the priority list lately. June's house was always immaculate. My bedroom had to be giving her gas.

"Well, yes," she said as she expertly made my bed. "But I also remember the Angels."

I wasn't following. "You mean when they gave me back your soul?"

"No, not that part," she said, picking up my dirty clothes and dropping them into the hamper. "When my soul was with Clarissa. They were there."

A cold chill swept through my body. I was furious. "Are you sure?"

"I am," June replied, staring out of the window. "When Gabe spoke directly to me, I recalled him shouting."

"Shouting what?"

June sighed and sat down on the edge of my newly made bed. "I'm not sure. When I'm near them, it seems to come back in bits and pieces." She paused then shuddered. "I'm not sure they can be trusted, Daisy."

Not what I wanted to hear since I didn't have much time to get them to forgive my father, but sadly, it wasn't surprising. Angels were not the finest of people in my experience.

"Can you remember if they were in on it with her?"

"In on what?" June asked.

"Right," I said with a sigh as I sat down on the edge of the bed next to her. "How much did Charlie explain to you?"

"That could take days for me to share, and I didn't

understand half of it. What helped me come to terms the most is that Tim told me he could make me look the way I used to so I can see my children and grandchildren."

I nodded. "Tim explained it was temporary?"

"He did," June confirmed, trembling and swiping at a tear. "I have to say it's all a bit overwhelming."

"That's one way to put it," I said, putting my arm around my dear friend. "I can't believe how calm you are. I thought I was losing my mind when I found out I was living with deceased squatters."

June raised a brow and gave me a wry smile. "Trust me, the breakdown is right around the corner. However, it will have to wait. Charlie explained a bit about what you have to do in the next three days."

"And how much did he tell you about me?"

"Not much."

"Quick question," I said, scooting up to the top of the bed and patting the spot next to me.

"Shoot," June replied, crawling up and joining me.

"Can you see the ghosts?"

She shook her head. "No. I wish I could."

I wished she could too. Gram would love to chat with June again. The fact that June couldn't see the dead most likely meant that she was more human than Immortal.

"Alrighty then, you ready to hear my farked-up story?"

June laughed. "Daisy, right now you could tell me that you turn into a flower and I'd believe you. I'm a fifty-seven-year-old woman in my twenty-five-year-old body. The love of my life is so old, I can't even comprehend it. Practically everyone I hold dear is not who I believed them to be and I still hold all of them close to my heart. I have a heck of a lot to get used to, but I have my Charlie. And at the age I landed when you gave me back my life, I get him for many more years than I thought I would."

"Oh my God," I said, staring at her like she'd grown an extra head. "You are so much more well-adjusted than I am."

She winked. "I'm older."

"Coulda fooled me," I shot back.

"I'm thinking not much can fool you, my dear," June said, resting her head on my shoulder. "Tell me your story. I have a feeling I need to hear it."

~

"My goodness," June said with a giggle, "I feel like I just listened to the plot of a blockbuster movie and the sequel then the TV series made from the movies."

"I wish," I said with an exhausted sigh.

In the two hours it had taken to lay out the synopsis of my new reality, June had hung on every word. She'd cried and I'd joined her when I told her about Steve. She been thrilled that Gram was still with me and that I had my mom and dad too. But the part that made her sob happy tears was when I told her all about the pregnancy.

"Have you picked out names?" she asked, reaching for anything remotely normal after what she'd been through and the story she'd just heard.

I didn't blame her. I searched for normal all the time.

"Mini-Daisy or Gideonia," I told her with a straight face.

I was a horrible liar, but I'd clearly pulled one over on June. She was so sweet that she was an easy target.

"Oh heavens." Her face scrunched. She looked like she'd swallowed a lemon. "I don't see you as someone who would want a mini-me. And Gideonia... that's just awful. I mean... unless you love it. Actually, it's a very nice name." She was backtracking. June didn't like to say anything unless she had something nice to say. The heat rose from her neck and landed on her cheeks. "I think Gideonia would be lovely—very unusual and... umm... meaningful."

"It sucks all kinds of butt," I said with a laugh.

She punched my arm. "You're just terrible," she chastised me with massive relief in her voice. "I thought I'd put my foot in it for a second there."

"Nope," I said, rolling off the bed. "I'd name her Ima Pig before I named her Gideonia."

"I can top that," June said with a giggle.

"Top that name," I told her, picking up the dirty clothes she'd missed and tossing them into the hamper. I was pretty sure some of them were clean, but for the life of me I couldn't tell. It would be embarrassing to explain to June why clean clothes were strewn all over the place. If it was on the floor it went into the hamper.

"Anna Conda," she said with a grin.

I laughed. "Good one. How about Dinah Soars?"

June fell back on the pillow in a fit of giggles. "Nice, but I'd go with Sue Flay."

"Ahhh, I see you've got game," I said, tossing a throw pillow at her. "How about Iona Frisbee?"

"Or Anne Teak?"

"Kerry Oki," I countered.

"I have an inappropriate one," she whispered.

"You?" I asked in mock horror. "Inappropriate?"

June's face grew pinker. "Yes… Betty Humpder."

"Oh my God," I shouted and jumped back onto the bed. "That's the nastiest thing I've ever heard you say in all the years I've known you."

June was blood red now and giggling like a fool. "I know," she wheezed out. "Soooo unlike me. But I have to credit my daughter. When she was pregnant, she came to the house and informed us she was naming her daughter Betty Humpder Wilson. We were simply speechless. She let us think that was our grandbaby's name for weeks!"

"What did Charlie say?" I asked, trying to imagine it.

"He was flabbergasted. Not a single word crossed his lips the entire time she was pulling our leg," she said, wiping away tears of laughter.

"Please tell me you got her back."

"We most certainly did," June informed me with a sly smile. "When the baby was born, we dropped off a huge basket of embroidered blankets, bibs and onesies for the baby at the hospital. Betty Humpder Wilson was in bright pink all over everything. Took me a month to monogram all of that. Of course, we made sure that we announced to anyone who would listen what our daughter had named her baby."

"What's the baby's actual name?" I asked, wondering if I could punk my mom and dad with a name for my little girl.

June smiled with true happiness. "It's Sarah. Sarah June Wilson—one of the true lights of my life along with my practical-joke-playing daughter. Want one more silly name?"

"Is it anything close to Betty Humpder?" I asked with a raised brow.

"No," June said, still a little pink in the face. "It's sweet—very nature-y like Daisy. Olive Branch."

I froze. Not because I wanted to name the little peanut in my stomach Olive Branch, but because it hit me in the gut. Hard.

"Forgiveness," I said softly. "What does forgiveness mean to you?"

June looked pensive for a moment. "Gandhi said, 'The weak can never forgive. Forgiveness is the attribute of the strong.'"

"Gandhi was a smart man," I said, wondering how strong the Angels were.

"I agree," June said, getting off the bed and straightening it. "To me, forgiveness doesn't mean condoning or excusing the wrong. And it doesn't minimize or even justify the crime. You can forgive someone without excusing the act. It's not the same as reconciling. I mean, that could certainly follow, but you can forgive without reestablishing a connection with the one you choose to forgive."

"But what if someone wants revenge instead of trying to forgive?" I asked, hoping June didn't walk into my bathroom. It was a shitshow in there.

June paused. "According to my mom, God rest her soul, the best revenge is to be unlike the one who performed the offense. It's what I taught my kids their entire lives. I live by it. Much easier to be nice."

I let her words sink in. It was anyone's guess if my siblings would forgive my father. It was a convoluted mess, not to mention, he hadn't known who they were—only that they existed. The argument would be that he could have searched for them, but he'd been forbidden by the Heavenly Higher-ups… whoever they were.

Wait. Was there actually anything to forgive? Was it just that I was grasping at straws to fulfill my task? Was I sprinting towards a dead end?

Crap. Thinking was hurting my brain.

Too bad, so sad. An aching brain was much better than losing my world as I knew it.

"I have it all wrong," I said, pressing the bridge of my nose with the palm of my hand.

"You have what all wrong?" June asked.

"The Angels don't need to forgive my dad," I explained.

"I'm not following, but keep going. Talk it out. You're doing great. You've got this," June insisted with a thumbs up and a smile.

I grinned and shook my head. June was the best cheerleader in the Universe. She had my back even though she had no clue what I was talking about. "It's circumstantial—my father not knowing about them. He was forbidden to search by whoever's in charge. There's nothing to forgive. My guess is that wouldn't cut it with Zadkiel, the cryptic asshead."

June nodded, completely lost but there for me all the way. "You have another idea?"

"I do," I said. "It's going to be ugly."

"How ugly?"

"Umm... seriously ugly," I replied with a shudder. "Candy Vargo did something heinous to the Angels and they need to forgive her... or she needs to forgive them."

"So you just have to oversee forgiveness to earn your spot as the Angel of Mercy?" June asked, trying to keep up.

"I think so," I told her, unlocking the door and opening it. "Oh, and I can't be judgmental. I have to stay neutral no matter what Candy Vargo did to the Angels."

"Can you do that?" she asked, following me as I hurried down the stairs.

I stopped. "Would you say it's judgmental if I puke when I find out what she did?"

June winced. "That might look a little judgey," she said. "If you feel iffy, just picture everyone in their underpants. I always find that helps when I'm nervous."

"Seriously?" I asked, squinting at her. "That helps?"

June nodded. "Makes me giggle. Might keep you from hurling."

It was doubtful, but I was taking any advice I could get. Even bad advice.

CHAPTER TEN

Everyone was in the living room. It was a large, airy space, but it felt like it was closing in around me. Heather and Missy had brought in a few chairs from the kitchen so everyone had somewhere to sit. They'd also set up a folding table on the far end near the foyer and loaded it down with food for all. No one had touched it except Candy Vargo. Nothing seemed to mess with Candy's appetite.

The Angels were still seated close to each other on the couch. They were awkward and uneasy. My dad stood by the fireplace eyeing them with suspicion as my mom floated next to him. A concerned expression marred her beautiful ghostly face.

Candy Vargo, Sister Catherine and Tim were squeezed together on the oversized armchair. Tim had his notebook out and his pen poised to write. Charlie and June sat on kitchen chairs, while Heather and Missy stood in the archway between the rooms.

Gideon sat silently on the stairs with Donna and Karen at his feet, his elbows resting on his jean-clad knees and his chin in his hands. His eyes roved the room missing nothing. His posture might have been casual, but his demeanor was tense. It matched everyone else's.

Only Gram was carefree, flying around and making sure everyone was comfortable. Her Southern hostess genes were showing. At least someone's were. Mine had gone AWOL.

Of course, the most silent object in the room was the loudest. The hourglass on the coffee table continued to spill golden sand from the Celestial Dunes and whittle away at the time I had left to prove I was worthy of the job I didn't really want.

"Okay," I said, pacing my living room in a slight panic. I found I couldn't make eye contact with anyone since I kept picturing them in their underpants. As much as I loved June, I was no longer going to her for advice. "I was wrong about the Angels forgiving my dad… and theirs."

"Damn straight," Prue said with a disgusted eye roll. "The Archangel doesn't deserve our forgiveness."

"And you're a hot mess of ugly rude," I snapped at her. My guess was that she wore a thong. "I was wrong because no forgiveness is due, on your part *or* his. The Archangel Michael has done nothing wrong. He was as much a victim as the four of you and Heather."

"Cry me a river, bitch," Abby said with sarcasm dripping off every word.

Gram zipped across the room and got in Abby's face. "You're makin' my butt itch," she shouted, wagging her finger at the stunned Angel. "If you don't watch that mouth, I'm gonna cream yer corn."

Abby glanced over at her sister, who was grinning.

"And you," Gram snapped, turning her attention to Prue. Prue's smile disappeared quickly. "You're about as useless as a screen door on a dang submarine—just uppity and nasty. You're gonna have a real hard time in life with that attitude."

"Angels are like hemorrhoids," Candy Vargo commented, pointing her toothpick at the foursome, who sank lower in their seats. "Pain in the ass when they come down for a visit and always a dang relief when they go back up."

Gram rolled her eyes. "Now that wasn't real nice, Candy Vargo. I'm disappointed in you."

Candy groaned. "I didn't say fuck one single time."

Gram tsked. "Tellin' people that they're a swollen vein in the region of the anus is not what a lady says."

"Thirty seconds ago, I was hungry," Heather said with a pained laugh. "Now? Not so much."

"Word," I muttered, agreeing with her. I glanced over at the Angels, who looked wildly unsure of how to proceed. Again, they pulled at my heart. Again, they didn't deserve that from me. "How much do you know about your creation?" I asked them.

"We weren't created," Rafe said, giving my father an icy glare. "We were born."

"You have mothers?" I pressed, wondering if their experience had been different than Heather's was.

Not one said a word. The answer was clear. They didn't have mothers.

"No mommy issues?" Heather inquired with a raised brow. "Just daddy issues?"

"No *issues* at all," Abby said with a shrug. "None."

I shook my head. "Well, we have something in common," I told Abby.

"Please, do share," she said in a snarly tone.

"We're both bad liars."

Gabe sighed and looked at the other three with sadness and regret. "We know we were born. We have no mother or father. We were trained together since birth. We're related without being a family. It was forbidden. There was no love. No kindness. We've led lives of loyalty, service and violence."

I exchanged a loaded glance with Heather. She was melting just a little bit as well. The Archangel Michael seemed unmoved. My father could be a difficult nut to crack. And the Angels weren't exactly helping themselves in the matter.

"There was a group created—kind of like thoroughbred horses—no sexual intercourse involved. It was done to streamline the species. You four and Heather are the result. Very unethical," I said.

"May I?" Heather asked me.

I nodded.

"We're petri dish Angels—not created and not born in a traditional way," she said flatly. "Yes, it was unethical. It was explained to me something like this—we're all aware there are shades of gray around every corner, especially for those who can't die. There are many circumstances of which we have no control—like the creation of Super Angels, for lack of a better way to describe us. Michael didn't know that we were the products of the experiment until a century ago, and he was forbidden to reach out."

"Yet, he did to you," Rafe pointed out coldly.

"Because I asked," Heather said.

"And he answered you?" Gabe questioned.

"Yep. And I punched him in the face," Heather replied.

"Same," I said. "I mean, I have a mother. And I feel awful about breaking his nose. He was protecting me from Clarissa's wrath and keeping my mom's soul safe."

"Is that on the table?" Gabe asked with a laugh. "Punching Pappy?"

God, I so wanted to like Gabe.

"Only if it is earned," my father said with no emotion in his tone. "Daisy and Heather earned the right to maim me. None of you have. And I have my doubts you ever will."

"Harsh," Candy Vargo said with a thumbs up to my dad. "I like your style, old man."

My father ignored her. I, on the other hand, did not. "Moving on," I said, walking over to Candy and standing in front of her.

She sighed dramatically. "What the hell did I do now?"

"Not sure," I admitted. "Do you owe the Angels forgiveness or do they owe you forgiveness?"

The Keeper of Fate turned a little green in the face. The Angels literally squeaked then gasped in horror—even the men. I felt the bile rise in my throat. What in the heck had gone down between them?

Closing my eyes and already regretting bringing the subject up, my mind went back to the conversation with June. I tried to remember exactly what she'd said about forgiveness. That was my goal and my mission. I was going to get someone to forgive someone if it was the last dang thing I did. At this point it was looking like it might be. Unfortunately, forgiveness was not what my brain decided to embrace.

"Daisy is guessing that Prue and Abby are wearing thongs—black like their hearts," I announced. "Daisy knows for a fact that Gideon is going commando. He left his underpants at the new house in the baby nursery after a few rounds of great banging. She's trying very hard not to think about her dad's underpants. While she's forty, it's still gross to acknowledge that parents have genitals. If she had to, she would speculate Rafe wears tighty-whities that match his pinched, assholey demeanor. Gabe is a bit looser in the personality department, so Daisy's opinion is that he's sporting light blue boxers. Candy Vargo is possibly wearing dirty purple underpants inside out. Daisy did this a few times in college when she didn't have time to do laundry. Candy Vargo has no housekeeping skills, so it's a safe bet to assume she doesn't do laundry all that much. June is wearing pink bikini underpants. Daisy knows this because she lent them to her. It's entirely reasonable to believe Charlie is wearing gray boxer briefs that belong to Gideon. The Grim Reaper wears boxer briefs when he's not going commando. Heather and Missy are boy briefs all the way. Daisy has two pairs of boy briefs and loves them. That leaves Tim. Daisy guesstimates that Tim wears starched white boxers—possibly with the postal service emblem on them."

There was a moment of silence. It was terrifying.

Then came the laughs. Hard laughs. Loud laughs. Laughs that made me want to disappear.

"Oh my freaking God," Heather shouted, doubled over in hysterics. "Where did *that* come from?"

"Where did *what* come from?" I asked with an awful sinking feeling in my stomach.

"Holy cow, Daisy," Missy said, grinning from ear to ear. "That was a little kinky."

Half of the people in the room were laughing and half were in shock with their mouths hanging open. Glaring at the hourglass, I wanted to melt into the floor.

"What did I say?" I asked in a choked whisper to Gideon, who shook his head and gave me a lopsided grin.

"I don't think you want to know."

"Oh dear," June said, covering her face in embarrassment. "I fear this is my fault. I told Daisy if she was worried about vomiting to picture everyone in their underpants to calm herself."

"Did it work?" Tim inquired, jotting down the ongoing mortifying action as it unfolded. "Are you calmer? And just to clarify, I do indeed starch my boxers, but I never wear white. Always sunny yellow boxers for me. No postal service emblem, but I like that touch. I shall address it immediately."

"Shit," I said, looking down and staring at my running shoes. I'd never wanted to run away so badly. "I'm... umm... sorry. I'm not exactly sure what horrid things I just said, but

I sincerely apologize. The hourglass likes to speak through me."

"Inaccurate," Prue said with the smallest hint of a smile on her usually surly mouth. "Zadkiel said the hourglass is not speaking through you. And my thong is peach, not black."

"Zadkiel is a dick," I said, then slapped my hand over my mouth and hoped he wasn't keeping tabs on my progress. While I stood by my statement, it was rude to say it aloud… and possibly deadly.

"That's a given," Gideon agreed. "However, while he is untrustworthy, he doesn't usually lie."

"So it's not the hourglass?" I asked in my outside voice, starting to come a little unhinged. "I'm just possessed?"

"You really left yourself wide open there," Abby said, biting back a nasty response with extreme effort.

"Go for it," I said, throwing my hands in the air. "Maybe you'll give me a clue mixed in with your bitchiness."

She sighed and refused to speak. The punishment Gideon had laid out in graphic detail was probably forefront in her mind.

"Sounds like your subconscious," Missy said, searching for the logic in the magic. "Definitely someone who knows you well and is in tune."

I looked at my BFF. "You think it's Steve?"

"No," my mother said with a surprised smile on her face. "I think it might be someone a little closer to home right now."

"Like a Guardian Angel?" I asked.

"So to speak," she said, floating over to me. "I had something similar happen to me once upon a time."

I touched her face. Having her with me was a miracle and we'd barely spent any time alone together. "Someone spoke through you?"

"Not exactly," she said, kissing the top of my head. "Someone sent me messages in my mind."

"When?"

She smiled. "A little over forty years ago."

My hands immediately went to my stomach. I would swear I felt something move inside me. "Me? I sent you messages?"

She nodded. "At times, very silly."

"And you think Mini-Daisy Gideonia is speaking through me? Embarrassing the heck out of me?"

"Oh hell no," Gabe said, letting his blond head fall forward. "That can't be the name you've chosen."

"It's NOT," I shouted with an eye roll. "It's a placeholder. I have a few others I'm leaning toward. I like Doris Shutt, Tish Hughes and Jenny Tull. Happy now?"

Gideon roared with laughter. Even the Angels couldn't help but smile. Heather, Missy, Charlie and June joined in on the laughs. My father looked a bit unsure if I was serious or not, but my mother's peal of giggles assured him that I hadn't completely lost my mind... yet.

"Have you considered Ima Hogg or Ura Pecker?" Tim asked with a silly grin. "They're real names."

"Yes, those were in consideration, but Helen Back beat it out until I decided that Hell in my daughter's name was probably a bad plan considering her lineage," I replied with a wink.

"Fuuuuuuuneeeah," Sister Catherine screamed as she giggled uncontrollably.

"I vote for Fonda Dicks," Candy Vargo announced.

"While that has a nice ring to it, my daughter might be gay," I pointed out. "I don't want to make her insecure about who she is and who she loves by relegating her to only being fond of male parts."

"I love you," Heather said, grabbing me and hugging me. "You're right out of your ever-loving, very open and forward-thinking mind."

"Thank you," I said, curtseying to the group. "I try."

"So, this is what happiness looks like?" Gabe asked, amazed as he glanced around the room at the smiling faces. "It's quite unusual."

My heart hurt for Gabe. It actually hurt for all four of them. Patting my stomach and hoping my little bean was done speaking for me, I realized a hard truth. Zadkiel wasn't telling me to forge forgiveness with others. He wanted *me* to forgive. Unfortunately, the one who had wronged me the most wasn't alive anymore.

And even if she was, I wasn't sure I could forgive her. Ever.

"Second time today I was wrong," I said, walking over to the couch and standing in front of my two brothers and two sisters who I barely knew. "Forget about whatever happened between you and Candy Vargo."

"I wish I could," Rafe said with a shudder.

"If you all want to work that out, it's on you, not me," I

told them. "I have a different plan now. I'm going to forgive you and we're going to get along."

Abby rolled her eyes. "Good luck with that."

She had a point, but I had a plan.

"Well, butter my butt and call me a biscuit," Jennifer yelled as she walked through the front door, letting the cold air in with her entrance. "Sweet baby Jesus in cleats! June, who did your plastic surgery? My God, you look twenty-five-years-old!"

"Jennifer!" Tim squealed in a panic, sprinting across the room so fast he hit the wall and knocked himself out.

"For the love of everything fuckin' idiotic," Candy Vargo griped, walking over to Tim and pouring a glass of water on his head. "Wake up, douchebag."

"Jennifer," Tim mumbled, coming to. "Not supposed to be here."

Jennifer helped her buddy to his feet and checked his eyes for dilation. "Tim, you hit that durn wall so hard, your brain should have fallen out of your ears. Good thing the human brain is sixty percent fat. Probably cushioned that smackdown you just had with the wall. Did you know if you ate your brain, it would have a similar consistency to bean curd?"

"In Chinese cuisine, eating brains is considered a delicacy," Tim said, not to be outdone by Jennifer's stomach-churning knowledge. "It's often cooked in spicy hot pot or barbecued."

"Human brains?" I gagged out.

"Hell to the no," Jennifer said. "Pig brains. And in India, goat brains."

"Correct," Tim said with a weak smile, still woozy.

"I'm never eating again," Heather said.

"Jennifer, what are you doing here?" Tim asked, dazed but concerned for her safety.

"I'm supposed to be here, Timmy," she said with a laugh. "Daisy invited me for a booze-free lunch. From the looks of it, I'm gonna say I'm late. And seriously June, who did your work and when the hell did you get it done? I mean, I know I was drunk the other day, but day-yum, you look great!"

"Umm…" June wrung her hands nervously and looked desperately to Charlie for help. He quickly changed his age back to what Jennifer would remember. She hadn't noticed him yet since she'd been so fixated on June.

"You can tell me your secret later," Jennifer told her, hoisting Tim up into her arms like he was a baby.

Jennifer was tiny but strong. Tim was tall and skinny. They looked absurd.

"You can put me down. I'm fine," Tim insisted, mortified.

"No can do," Jennifer said. "I'm thinkin' you might have a concussion. Gonna need to keep an eye on you."

She settled herself on the loveseat with Tim on her lap like he was her little dog. Patting his head, she looked around the room. Her expression grew confused as she scanned the occupants.

The Angels tensed. Abby hissed and Prue growled quietly. I was so close to caging them, I could taste it. But that might send Jennifer over the edge. She was my main concern. I was thankful she wasn't wearing her glasses. If she got a good look at June, she'd freak. No plastic surgery could do to June what magic had done.

"Do I know you?" Jennifer asked, squinting at the Angels. "I could swear I know you people."

Gabe shot the others a look that made me almost swallow my tongue. His admission about being raised in violence was very clear and obvious. If it had been aimed at Jennifer instead of his siblings, I would have dropped a barrier faster than a heart could pound out a beat.

"Do nothing," Gabe hissed under his breath.

"Fuck you," Rafe whispered back. "Rules are rules."

"Humans can't know," Prue muttered.

Moving so fast I probably went invisible for a hot sec, I put my body between them and my dear buddy who knew far more than she was spelled to forget.

How?

Not a clue.

Jennifer set Tim on the floor and peeked around me as Gideon walked over and stood next to me. His silent warning was loud and clear.

"Were you people in *Twilight*? You just look so dang familiar. You were the Illuminati, right? That has to be it! You were fantastic! Scary as all get out."

"How does she remember?" Prue demanded, shocked.

Jennifer grinned. "I've seen it at least twenty times," she admitted sheepishly. "Great work, kids."

"Seen what?" Abby snapped, standing up and narrowing her eyes.

"*Twilight*," Jennifer answered, grabbing Tim's notebook from his hand. "Can I get your autographs?"

"Unacceptable," Abby snarled, raising her hands above her head.

I didn't hesitate. I didn't say a word. There was no time. With a grunt and a dive, I tackled all four Angels. My arms were like steel bands wrapped around them.

And then I fell in. I fell into a ring of Hell that I wasn't aware I could visit.

And it sucked.

CHAPTER ELEVEN

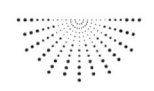

THE COLD. THE COLD WENT ALL THE WAY TO MY BONES AND TORE through my body like sharp, frozen daggers made of ice. Trying to catch my breath, I gasped for air and forced myself to stay calm.

The only sound that left my lips came from so far away I could barely hear it.

My head pounded violently and every single cell in my body screamed for oxygen. I attempted to reverse what was happening, but I was locked together with my angelic siblings in a deadly embrace.

How was this happening? They weren't dead. I only entered the minds of the dead—not the living. Had I just killed them when I jumped them? The thought was absurd, but I wasn't sure how else to explain what was happening.

My mind went numb and I couldn't feel my limbs anymore. I was no longer physically connected to the Angels.

"Oh my God," I muttered trying to acclimate to the freezing surroundings. "Am I dead too?"

A scream of fury echoed like a bomb through the vast nothingness. I was pretty sure it was Abby. It was followed by a string of curses that sounded distinctly like the voice of an outraged Rafe.

Slowly opening my eyes, I tried to peer through the heavy fog surrounding me. This was different than what I was used to. Every other time I dove into the minds of the dead, the minute I opened my eyes, I could see clearly.

Today? Not at all. But then again, I wasn't sure anyone here was dead.

"Where am I?" Prue shrieked.

"This might be Hell," Gabe said, sounding strangely calm. "Nothing less than what we deserve."

"My afterlife can't be spent with you cretins," Abby hissed. "I can't see a damn thing."

"Stop touching me," Prue snarled.

The sounds of slapping and hissing assaulted my eardrums. I supposed it was better than them electrocuting each other.

"This is that bitch's fault," Abby snarled. "I will destroy her. Clarissa had said she would be the end of us. I should have believed her."

"We set Daisy up to fail," Prue reminded everyone harshly. "She has less than seventy-two hours to prove otherwise. She will not. Time will reverse itself. Clarissa will be back as the Angel of Mercy. If we'd gone against her, it would be far worse for us."

"Have you considered the thought that there might be no more us?" Gabe inquired. "Look around, Prue. Take it in."

"Take what in?" she snapped. "I can't see a damn thing."

"Holding back the soul of Daisy's friend and forcing her to become the Angel of Mercy was positively inspired," Rafe commented with a ruthless chuckle. "In the end, we will win. We always have and we always will."

My blood ran cold and I wanted to throw up. Imagining everyone in their underpants would not help. While June had been wrong about the calming underpants method, she had been correct that the despicable Angels had conspired with Clarissa. They believed they had set me up to fail and that they would win. However, victory in the short term wasn't necessarily a triumph in the end.

"Shut up," Gabe roared. "Clarissa was insane and we fucked up. If we'd stolen the soul back and returned it, we would not be in this mess."

"Mess is not exactly the word that comes to mind," Rafe said flatly.

"How do we get out of here?" Prue screamed in a frustrated rage.

"Who says we're getting out?" Gabe asked. "Zadkiel warned us that the price of our crimes would be high."

"So this is it?" Prue demanded. "We're stuck in a foggy Hell for the rest of time?"

"Apparently," Rafe said.

I hoped not. I didn't have the time to hang out with soulless imbeciles for eternity. This was not business as usual. My mind raced with thoughts on what to do. It came up empty. Could I leave without them?

If I pictured myself back in my living room, would my departure damn them to this nothingness?

Did I really care?

Unfortunately, yes.

Why? I wasn't sure.

I might be the reason for my own downfall. The Angels may indeed win in the end. But I wasn't going down without a fight.

"Open your eyes," I said in a cold voice.

"What?" Abby hissed.

"I said, open your eyes. NOW."

With a wave of my hand, the fog cleared. There was no floor or walls to speak of. We stood in a circle of gray nothingness—a vast landscape of oblivion, a colorless void.

Not one Angel said a word. I watched them as they tried to figure out how much I'd heard.

"Speak now. You have one chance to free yourselves or I'll leave you here," *I said, so calmly even Abby blanched.*

"You can do that?" *Rafe questioned, looking skeptical.*

I simply stared at him. I had no clue if I could, but that was not public information. If being cryptic and vague was the way of the Angels, I could play that game.

Glancing down at my watch, I pressed my lips together. I was fully aware that time ran differently here. There was no telling how much time had passed in the "real" world. It felt as if we'd only been here for a few minutes, but that could be deceiving.

Considering I didn't have a ton of time to lose, it was "time" to play ball.

"We can do this the hard way or the easy way," *I said.* "You talk or I dive deeper into you."

"Are we dead?" *Gabe asked.*

I shrugged. "I don't know."

No one liked that answer—including me. "However, if you are, it might be a good time to repent."

"To you?" *Abby shouted.* "Repent to you? I don't think so."

Again, I shrugged. She was such a horrid piece of work. "Honestly, I don't care what you do. As Zadkiel said, the price for your crimes is up to you."

"And you will be the judge?" Prue asked emotionlessly.

Zadkiel's words danced in my mind and twisted with June's. He'd told me that judgment would be my savior or my downfall. Who was I to judge anyone? I had to play the long game even if winning in the moment would feel great. Forgiving those who deserved it the least was my mission. June had said that forgiveness didn't mean condoning or excusing the wrong. And it didn't minimize or even justify the crime. I could forgive someone without excusing the act.

I was the Angel of Mercy. Could I show these virtual strangers who were related to me mercy? The four people who would delight in my failure and demise?

Was my mission standing before me? I was about to find out.

"Touch me," I told Gabe. "Take my hand."

In my mind, he was the only one worth saving. But again, who was I to judge?

He reached out to me. I took my brother's hand in mine. To my shocked surprise, Prue approached me with her hand outstretched. I took it immediately.

Abby and Rafe watched with undecipherable expressions.

"One chance," I repeated. "Take the hands of your brother and sister. Connect with me."

"Or?" Abby's eyes narrowed to slits.

"I have no idea," I told her truthfully. "But if I don't know you, I can't forgive you."

"Not sure you will be able to forgive us if you know us," Rafe said, taking Prue's free hand in his own.

"I would rather die than be forgiven by you," Abby said,

turning her back on us and walking into the fog. "You are scum. I am the law."

"Hang on a sec," I said, disengaging from Prue and Gabe. Sprinting after the quickly retreating Abby, I grabbed her by the hair, threw her to the ground and sat on her. Nice Daisy wasn't going to cut it. That was fine. I was digging deep for Take No Bullshit Daisy—Angel Style. Abby understood might over right. There was no love lost between us, but if I was going to get out of here, all of them were coming with me.

As Zadkiel suggested, I was keeping my friends close and my enemies closer.

Abby grunted in anger and tried to throw me off of her.
She failed.

Holding her down and getting in her face, I smiled. It wasn't a pleasant smile. "It's all for one and one for all," I said. "You will join us or I will make you. You feel me?"

"You can't," she spat.

"Watch me," I shot back, waving my hand and trapping her in glistening golden chains. The only parts of her body that could move were her eyes and her mouth. After she spewed more filth at me than I'd ever heard in my life, I reached into my pocket and pulled out a tube of superglue. I was amazed that it had made the trip.

"You have a choice," I said, twisting off the cap. "You can voluntarily shut your nasty piehole or I can do it for you."

"Die, bitch!" she shouted.

"Alrighty then," I said, covering her lips in the glue and holding them shut.

If we made it out of here, she was going to have a hell of a time removing the glue—might even have to cut off her lips. I didn't care. Plus, from all I'd witnessed, Immortals could regrow body parts.

"Join me," I called out to the others. "Quickly."

"Why are you doing this?" Prue asked, confused.

"Doing what?" I asked, taking her hand and Gabe's in mine.

"Saving her," Rafe clarified, clasping Prue's hand. "I wouldn't."

"Neither would I," Prue added.

I rolled my eyes. "What is wrong with you people? It's the right thing to do. I may never like any of you. In fact, I'm pretty sure I won't, but I can forgive the transgressor without condoning the sin."

"And holding our hands will accomplish what?" Gabe asked, glancing down at our clasped hands.

I hoped to the darkness and back I wouldn't regret what I was about to do. The choices were pretty limited. "I need to know you. I can't forgive you if I don't know you. If I touch you, I can see your memories."

"We don't deserve your forgiveness," Prue said.

"Not your decision," I replied. "Close your eyes. All of you."

They complied. Even Abby. That was a relief since I didn't want to superglue her eyes shut. It was bad enough that I'd glued her lips together.

I wasn't sure that I could dive into four minds at once, but they'd been together since birth. If I could see one person's memories, there was a good chance I'd see all of them in the memories.

The sensations were what I remembered. I was back in familiar territory. Pictures raced across my vision so quickly I couldn't make them out. It was like an old static-filled, black-and-white TV screen inside my head. Finally, it slowed.

However, while I recognized what was happening, I'd never

seen horror like this in the minds of the dead. My breath caught in my throat and I swallowed back the deep sadness that consumed me.

Everything I was seeing had already happened. There was nothing I could do to change it.

Vicious beatings of all four by faceless beings flashed across the screen over and over. I saw them as terrified children and as cold, angry teens. How was this Heavenly? Why had this been allowed to happen?

I watched the adult versions of Abby and Prue huddled together as Rafe and Gabe were harshly punished. Lightning flashed, thunder cracked and blood flowed.

"You shall absorb the sins of humanity," a voice bellowed as my siblings cowered in fear.

"No," Abby screamed right before a switch lashed her face.

"Silence," the disembodied voice demanded. "You were created for this reason. Accept your lot. In the end it will be easier."

There was nothing easy about what I was watching. The screen in my mind was awash with blood and agony. My siblings had come from abuse and violence. It was what they knew. Only small glimpses of a gentle hand appeared every so often. They craved the benevolent attention, but it was far outweighed by brutality.

How they were even semi-functional was beyond me. Someday I would find who did this and make them pay. The only instinct these Angels had was the survival instinct.

"ENOUGH," I shouted.

Opening my eyes, I stared at the Angels. Not one made eye contact. Waving my hand, I removed the chains from Abby. I left the glue. Hearing her swear at me wasn't on the agenda.

"My heart breaks for all of you," I whispered brokenly. "I abhor the sins you committed against me, but I do not hate the sinners. You barely stood a chance. I don't know that I'll ever be able to love you but not because I don't want to try. But no one will love you until you are granted the opportunity to love yourselves. I forgive you. I forgive you and hope you will search for the grace to love yourselves."

Rafe was the first to drop to his knees. Gabe followed quickly. Tears fell from Prue's eyes and rolled down her cheeks. She slowly went to her knees and bowed her head. Abby closed her eyes. Her body shuddered uncontrollably. A small piece of my heart shattered for the woman who would have happily seen me die and had done her best to make it happen.

Maybe I was crazy. Or maybe I'd just felt true grace for the first time.

Abby dropped to her knees and pressed her forehead to the ground.

"Get up," I said. I didn't like them bowing to me. I was neither above or beneath them. "We're leaving. There's not much time left."

"We shall assist you," Rafe said.

The words were surprising coming from him. I would have expected Gabe to offer help. I was wary of all of them. I could forgive, but history, when dismissed, tended to repeat itself. Frankly, I wasn't sure my forgiveness would last very long if they betrayed me again.

"How?" I asked.

"We can manipulate time," Prue said. "We did it in the bookstore with you when we met."

They had. I'd forgotten. In my defense, a whole heck of a lot had happened since then. "You can buy me more than seventy-two hours? Well, not seventy-two anymore, but whatever I have left."

"No," Gabe said. "Stopping time will not slow the Celestial Sands in the hourglass, but we could send you backwards if it would be helpful."

I nodded. It really wasn't help at all, but the offer was appreciated. Plus, I was hopeful I'd accomplished my mission. I had truly forgiven those who had harmed me. Now I had to make sure they didn't harm anyone else.

I eyed them. "None of you will touch Jennifer. No casting spells. If she remembers, it's for a reason. As Candy Vargo would say, 'don't fuck with fate'. Are we clear on that?"

"Crystal," Prue said with a raised brow. "It's what landed us here. I'd rather not visit again anytime soon."

"Touch me," I instructed. "We're leaving."

"Should we click our heels three times?" Gabe asked with a small smile.

"Sure," I said. "Whatever floats your boat. Hang on. The ride might be bumpy."

"Trust me," Prue said. "We're used to bumpy."

From what I'd just seen, the statement was tragically true.

CHAPTER TWELVE

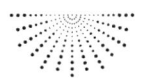

I opened my eyes to six glowing, deadly and furious Immortals standing over me and the Angels in my living room. We were in a pile on the floor in the same position that I'd tackled them in. My relief that we'd all made it back disappeared. I was clearly going to have to go to bat for the Angels again. Thankfully, Jennifer, June and Missy were nowhere in sight—neither were Gram, my mom or Sister Catherine. The scene in front of me could send Jennifer and the others into a nervous breakdown. I was pretty dang close myself.

Gideon's ebony-black wings had burst from his back and he was on fire. Literally. Crackling red flames surrounded him. The Grim Reaper looked like he'd walked right out of the bowels of Hell. However, my father, Charlie, Tim, Candy Vargo and Heather were no walk in the park.

Heather's skin danced with tattoos and her eyes were wild and unfocused. Her long, lean body was in a semi-crouched position, ready to attack. Tim didn't look all that different physically, but he'd paled to the point of ghostly and his eyes burned a sparkling, crazed green. He bared his teeth and made sounds that chilled me to the bone.

Charlie's eyes shot silver fire and his hands sparked with rage. His growl sounded animalistic and he looked as inhuman as I'd ever seen him. And then it got worse. I gasped aloud as I took in Candy Vargo. She was a stunningly terrifying creature with fangs and claws. She was the stuff nightmares were made of—and she looked hungry. A sick thought occurred to me. Had she eaten the Angels? Was that what none of them would talk about? I pushed the thought away as fast as it had arrived. I simply couldn't go there. Ever.

And my father… he was a blinding golden mass of fury. He was so bright in his rage it was difficult to look at him.

"Daisy," he roared, rocking the foundation of my farmhouse. "Move away from them. NOW."

"Listen to your father," Gideon growled, his eyes fixed on the Angels underneath me.

"Egos," I said, easing off the pile. Much to my father and Gideon's displeasure, I waved my hand and dropped a barrier around Prue, Abby, Rafe and Gabe. With a snap of my fingers, I also removed the glue from Abby's mouth. Risky, but it was the right thing to do. It would be horrifying to watch her cut her lips off. "Check your egos. I've got this under control."

"Daisy," my father ground out. "You have no idea what you're dealing with."

"Actually, I do," I said, standing up and motioning for everyone to take a step back. "I've forgiven them."

"Just like that?" Candy Vargo asked, perplexed and gnashing her sharp fangs.

"No," I said, backing up a little. "Not just like that. Somehow I ended up mind diving into them."

"Wait. Are they dead? I thought you could only mind dive into the dead," Tim said, peering through the barrier at the Angels.

"Good question. I wondered that myself," I told him. "And no. They're not dead."

"Damn shame," Candy muttered.

I held up my hand. "Nope," I said, staring her down even though she was freaking scary. "Not a damned shame. Their pasts have been a damned shame. They will receive a second chance. What they do with it is up to them."

No one moved. The people I adored looked at me like I'd finally gone and lost it. Maybe I had, but I was owning it.

"Says who?" Candy asked, picking her fangs with a toothpick.

"Says the Angel of Mercy," I shot back.

"This is getting *very* interesting," Tim said.

"What's been done to them is criminal," I said with an exhausted grimace. "It was inhuman. The fact that they have even a semblance of humanity left in them is a miracle."

"Define semblance," Gideon said, still eyeing the Angels like he was going to destroy them. "And humanity."

"Look," I told him, needing him to hear me. "They're not innocents by any stretch of the imagination. While I forgave them, I don't condone what they did."

"What exactly did they do? Besides the obvious of leaving you and Clarence to die by Clarissa's hand," Heather said, still crouched low.

"They set me up," I explained.

"To?" Gideon asked, finally moving his gaze to me. His expression was filled with so much pain that I found it hard to breathe.

"I love you," I told him.

"I died a thousand deaths today," he replied. *"Please do not ever do that again."*

I sighed. *"Wasn't planned. However, I promise not to do it on purpose."*

He nodded curtly.

"I don't want you to destroy the Angels," I said.

The Grim Reaper pressed the bridge of his nose in frustration. The fire around him abated and his wings folded and disappeared into his back. "Go on," he said so everyone could hear. "They set you up to what?"

"To fail. They didn't or still don't believe I'll pass Zadkiel's test. They had more fear of Clarissa than me. They held on to June's soul to give me no choice about agreeing to take the job as Angel of Mercy, knowing I would be tested and assuming I would fail."

"Traitorous," my father spat, turning his back on the four.

"Maybe," I agreed. "But they're willing to help me now. If I need any. Although, I'd think I've completed my mission."

All eyes shot to the hourglass. The golden sand was still streaming through the opening between the globes.

"Doesn't look like you nailed it yet." Candy Vargo pointed out the obvious.

"Son of a…" I hissed, running my hands through my hair and pulling my messy bun down. "How long was I out?"

"Ten hours," Heather said.

"Who do I have to forgive to catch a freaking break?" I shouted. "I'll be right back. No one harm the Angels."

Without a backward glance, I sprinted to the front yard. Cryptic bullshit wasn't working for me. I needed answers and I needed them now.

"Zadkiel," I shouted at the dark sky above. "Get your omitting ass down here."

I waited. Nothing happened.

"NOW," I demanded.

Still no Zadkiel.

Candy Vargo sauntered out into the yard. "Lemme show you how it's done."

"How what's done?"

"Watch and learn," she said with a wicked grin. Raising her middle fingers to the sky, she laughed. "Daisy, did you know that Zadkiel's pecker is crooked?"

"I'm sorry. What?" I choked out.

"Leans to the right. Hard to look at it when he gets it up. Pun intended."

I felt my stomach roil. I didn't want to piss the Angel off, I just wanted him to show up. "Umm… Candy, is this a good idea?"

"You want the son of a bitch here?"

"Yes," I answered.

"Then yep. It's a fine fuckin' plan." She stuck a toothpick

in her mouth and kept going. "Yes siree, he only has one nut and likes to wear women's panties."

"Seriously?" I asked, trying not to laugh. Candy Vargo was making it abundantly clear what had gone down between Zadkiel and her.

"Nah," she whispered, "but he's a macho, vain motherfucker. This'll kill him."

I expelled a long breath. I just hoped it didn't mean that when he showed up—if he showed up—he'd kill *us*.

"And get this," she shouted, enjoying herself immensely. "Zadkiel didn't retire, he got fired. That's right—got fired for stealing lunches from the Celestial Community Fridge… five hundred and seventy-two times."

"For real?" I asked.

"I exaggerated," Candy Vargo admitted. "It was four hundred times. They only caught him after they put laxatives in a vat of vanilla pudding. The bastard was on the crapper for a week. AND he's a man hooker. That slimy roamin' salami lies about bangin' floozies when he's supposed to be in a committed fuckin' relationship. PUN INTENDED AGAIN. That cheatin' dog is as windy as a sack full of farts."

"Are you quite finished?" Zadkiel roared, looking pissed off and horrified as he appeared in a blast of silver lightning that lit the night sky and a deafening crack of thunder.

"My work here is done," Candy Vargo announced, flipping Zadkiel off and walking back into the house.

The silent showdown made me regret calling on him for a moment. The Angel was seething. Granted, Candy Vargo had revealed some rather personal and embarrassing information.

"You rang?" Zadkiel ground out.

"I did," I replied. "I've completed my mission. You can take your hourglass home."

His brow arched and his lips curled. It was a dastardly look on him. "I don't think so."

I wanted to blast the Angel straight to the darkness. If I tackled him, could I enter his mind? Would the knowledge I needed be easier to get if I simply took it instead of asking for it?

"I'd table that thought," Zadkiel warned me. "If you go in, you may never come out."

"You can read my mind?"

"Only when you think loud," he replied, snapping his fingers.

His throne appeared. Seating himself, he crossed his huge arms over his chest and waited. He was an asshole of epic proportions.

"I forgave the Angels," I said.

"Congratulations," he replied in a bored tone.

Inhaling slowly and expelling my breath even slower, I tried to read the man. I couldn't. The game playing was getting old and the consequences of losing were catastrophic. If at first you don't succeed, try again. Play the player.

"Thank you," I replied politely.

He looked confused. My guess was that he expected me to throw a fit or beg. Not happening. Placing one hand on my stomach over the precious gift inside me, I snapped my fingers with my other hand. A golden throne, twice the size of Zadkiel's, appeared. I almost laughed at the gaudiness, but sucked it up and sat on it. Leaning back and getting comfortable, I smiled at the Angel.

"Much better," I said. "So did you really get fired for stealing food?"

His eyes narrowed dangerously. Zadkiel didn't reply.

"Kind of petty if you ask me. It surprises me that you can't make your own lunch," I said. "Although, the laxatives were inspired."

"What exactly are you trying to accomplish?" he asked.

I shrugged. "I'm getting to know you."

"That could take a while," he commented. "You don't have much time and you've lost quite a bit by calling me back."

"How much?" I asked.

"To be determined," he replied coolly.

"You want me to fail," I accused him as my stomach tightened and my body felt numb. "You want your job back. All of this is bullshit. You can have the job. I don't want it."

Zadkiel rolled his eyes. "If I wanted the job, I would still have it," he said in an icy tone. "And while I may or may not have pilfered a few lunches, I was *not* fired."

"Sure," I said, waving a dismissive hand. "Whatever you want to believe, dude. Knock yourself out."

Lightning exploded in the sky and the Angel growled. I didn't move a muscle. His theatrics didn't scare me. Clapping my hands, I dropped all the trees in the yard—the biggest narrowly missed crushing him and his silver throne. That was on purpose.

"Nice move," he replied, taking in the damage I'd just caused.

"Thanks, I have more where that came from," I said in a casual tone.

"Show me," he dared.

"I could do that, but I'm not sure you want me to."

"And might that be because you've already played your hand?" he inquired condescendingly.

I laughed. "Nope, not even close. The truth is I have no clue what I'm capable of. If you'd like to be my test subject, that works for me. I don't like you one bit, so I won't hold back. From what I understand, Immortals can grow back body parts. Soooo, if I accidentally remove a few it's no biggie, right? Just sit still," I directed. "I'd hate to incinerate my house. Oh, and is there a body part that you're especially fond of?" I held up my curled pinkie and wiggled it at him. "Possibly something crooked that you'd like me to avoid. Not sure I can promise I won't hit it, but I can try."

The Angel paled a bit. "Maiming me will not help you accomplish your goal," he snapped, quickly covering his privates with his hands.

"What will?" I shot back. "In a nonlinear, nonspecific, absolutely ridiculous way, I understand you're my advisor. You suck so far."

"Your compliments humble me."

"My guess is that nothing humbles you," I said calmly. "Narcissistic jackasses are difficult to humble in my experience."

The Angel threw his head back and laughed. "You don't fear me?"

"No. I fear losing what I love. I don't love you."

He silently considered what I'd said, then shrugged. "The loss is mine. From those who you have gathered close, your love seems like a precious gift indeed."

I wasn't sure what to do with that. My polite Southern side wanted to tell him that I would try to love him, but it would be a lie. Kind lies weren't really kind at all.

"Help me," I said. "If you're stealing my time, you owe me."

"According to whom?"

"Me," I said.

"And you are?"

I stared at him hard. I was Daisy Leigh Amara-Jones. I was the Death Counselor. But I was something more. I'd felt true grace in the minds of the Angels. I understood what it meant to forgive. Forgive the sinner, not the sin.

My body tingled and I knew my eyes blazed gold. Zadkiel was bathed in a golden haze. My heart pounded hard in my chest. I was about to speak my truth. "I am the Angel of Mercy. I forgive you," I said. "You should learn to forgive yourself as well. Always forgive, Zadkiel, but never forget. If you do, you'll be a prisoner of your own hatred and doomed to repeat your transgressions for eternity."

Zadkiel's chin dropped forward and a sound came from deep within him that reminded me of a wounded animal. I wondered if I'd gone too far, but I didn't care. I felt free. If the Angel chose to help me, fine. If not, I'd figure it out. I had to. The job was mine and I planned to keep it.

"Think hard, Angel of Mercy," he said quietly. "It's in front of you. Listen to your own words. They are prophetic.

You have to see it for yourself. I am not permitted to solve the puzzle for you. Go back over my words. Take what you have discovered and use it wisely. There is only one chance to succeed."

"Why did you retire?" I asked.

His gaze met mine. The amount of pain I saw in his expression was gut-wrenching. "I left before I became desensitized. It's a dangerous proposition to lose your humanity. It serves no one. I was smart enough to end my journey before my journey ended me."

"And you chose your successor," I pressed, refusing to say Clarissa's name out loud.

His expression hardened and his eyes narrowed. "Everyone makes mistakes."

"Umm... understatement."

"Let he or she who is without sin cast the first stone."

"Fine point, well made," I said, taking a line out of Gideon's book. "You're dismissed."

The look of shock on his face would have been funny if my existence as I knew it wasn't on the line. However, if he refused to help me, he was wasting valuable minutes that I couldn't afford to lose.

"Tell me how much time I have left," I said, not playing around.

"Twelve hours," he replied flatly.

I swallowed back a scream of fury. His desire to see me fail was too obvious to deny. I nodded jerkily. Standing up, I waved my hand. My throne disappeared and so did his. With his grand silver show of power gone, he found himself sitting on the cold, hard ground.

"You are not welcome here," I said in an icy tone. "Please leave."

He stood and nodded. "Remember that living forever is something that can destroy a mind. Have mercy on those who break."

On that last cryptic note, Zadkiel disappeared in a burst of silver light.

CHAPTER THIRTEEN

THE SCENE IN MY LIVING ROOM WAS SUCH A VAST juxtaposition to the one I'd just been in. I was gobsmacked. The Angels were in one piece and no longer inside the barrier. They sat quietly on the couch and watched the action unfold with baffled expressions.

No one was on fire. Candy Vargo no longer had fangs and claws and no one was glowing or sparking. June, Jennifer, Missy, my mom, Gram and Sister Catherine were back. The food table had been replenished and everyone was eating and chatting.

"Umm... I'm back," I said, uncertain what to do or say.

Sister Catherine mooned me and Candy flipped me off. Heather and Missy were making sure everyone had something to eat and drink. It was so normal it was surreal—normal being a relative term.

"How'd it go?" Jennifer asked, waving at me.

With no clue how to answer her, I shrugged. If she was

still clueless to the Immortal world around her, the truth wouldn't make sense.

"She remembers!" Tim announced with a smile. "Well, mostly."

"You bet your bippy I do," Jennifer said, slapping her buddy Tim on the back. "I still can't shake that all y'all aren't vampires, but the rest is coming back."

I sat down so I didn't drop to the floor. "How?"

"Well, now, I'm guessin' it's the Botox," she said, walking over and handing me a sandwich. "It's cheese, no meat."

"Thank you. Botox?" I asked, not following as I took a bite. Had the spell the Angels cast caused brain damage?

June giggled. "What we've determined is that all of the filler and Botox Jennifer has in her face helped deflect the spell."

"Yep," Jennifer said. "Of course, my boob job and butt lift probably served as a boomerang too."

"You've had a boob job?" I asked in somewhat of a daze. The Botox/filler/silicone boomerang saga was the most bizarre story I'd heard today, and I'd been through the story ringer.

"Darn tootin'," she said with a grin. "The girls were saggin' and needed a lift. I didn't want all you gals to ride my ass about the extra surgery so I conveniently forgot to mention the hooter improvement."

"Got it." I smiled. I didn't know it was possible anymore, but Jennifer was magical that way. "You remember *everything*?"

"She does, or some slightly off version of it," Heather said, shaking her head. "The dingbat has put in a request to have her soul stolen and reintroduced so she can look like June."

"Nope," I said, closing my eyes and wincing. "Not happening."

"We already told her you wouldn't go for that," Missy said, handing me a glass of lemonade.

Gideon stood quietly against the wall with his arms crossed over his chest. He watched me closely. I felt his gaze before I met it.

"Is it over?" he asked.

I shook my head. "No."

"Any clues how to proceed?" my father asked tightly.

"Cryptic ones," I told him. "I'm going to eat then figure it out. I need normal for a half hour."

"Business as usual," Gideon reminded me.

I nodded and took another bite of my cheese sandwich. I'd given up meat completely when my dead roommates had moved in. It kind of grossed me out. While a plain cold cheese sandwich was kind of boring, I was starving. It was delicious.

"Alrighty then," Jennifer bellowed. "I can feel a dang roll comin' on and I'm gonna go for it. Everybody ready?"

"For what?" Gabe inquired.

"For Hell on earth," Heather said.

"Should we take cover?" Prue asked, alarmed.

"Not that kind of hell," Tim assured the wary Angels. "More like Purgatory with visuals."

"Purgatory is real?" I asked with a mouthful.

"If you want it to be, then yes," Abby replied.

I had nothing to say to that, so I just kept eating. Religion was freaking bizarre.

Jennifer took a preemptive bow before grossing everyone out. "Eye boogers contain urine."

"I'm eating," Heather griped.

"Not anymore," June said with a pained expression, putting her sandwich back onto her plate.

"Correct," Tim confirmed. "Everyone pees a little out of their eyes."

"This is what humans do for fun?" Prue asked, confused.

"And Immortals," Tim told her. "Join in if you'd like."

Abby wrinkled her nose in disgust, but didn't look like she was on the verge of killing anyone. "I'll pass."

Gabe raised his hand. "I'd like to give it a try."

Rafe rolled his eyes. "Please don't."

"Turn that frown upside down, Mr. Angel-pants," Jennifer told Rafe. "Knowledge is power."

"Debatable," Heather muttered.

Gabe grinned and cleared his throat. "The average person passes wind fourteen times a day. Rafe expels gas at least a hundred times a day."

Rafe closed his eyes and groaned. "He who smelt it, dealt it."

"Excellent!" Tim said. "You'll fit right in here as long as you don't kill anyone. We frown upon random or unprovoked dismemberment and bloodshed. Anyhoo, seventy to ninety percent of the dust in your home contains dead skin cells, which means Candy Vargo's house is a literal skin cell museum."

"Fuck you," Candy said.

"What did you just say?" Gram shouted at her. "Can't get mad at the truth, girlie."

"Fine," Candy grumbled. "Eat me," she said to Tim.

The Angels blanched in horror. My morbid guess about what may have happened between them and Candy Vargo might be true. A change of subject was necessary or else I'd upchuck. And I refused to picture anyone in their grundies. That had gone poorly.

"Earwax is actually a type of sweat," I announced to the surprise of everyone—including myself. Desperate times called for unappetizing measures.

"Seriously?" Heather asked, appalled. "You're joining the club?"

"When in Rome…" I said with a laugh.

"I have one. I think," Prue said.

"Shoot," Jennifer told her.

"Shoot who?" she asked, looking around perplexed.

"Shoot no one," I said quickly. "It's an expression. It means it's your turn to talk."

The Angels exchanged bewildered glances. They had a tremendous amount to learn. They were as literal as Tim.

"Okay," Prue said. "There is no factual evidence that today is Thursday. We all just have to trust that someone kept track since the very first Thursday."

Everyone was silent while we mulled it over.

"Damn," Jennifer muttered. "Prue might have won this round. While it wasn't gross, it was definitely profound."

"I concur," Tim said. "Prue is the winner on this debatable Thursday."

"It's actually Friday," Abby pointed out. "It's after midnight."

"I stand corrected," Tim said. "On this debatable Friday."

My half hour of normal was over. Glancing around the room, I took a mental snapshot and stored it away. I loved these people. I hoped I'd be given the opportunity to love the Angels. I had less than twelve hours left to make that wish come true.

"Zadkiel took time away from me," I said.

Gideon swore and punched a hole in the wall. Charlie shifted right back to his inhuman-looking state and Candy Vargo's fangs popped out.

"How much time?" my dad asked as my mom gasped and began to fly in tight circles of anger.

"Less than twelve hours."

"What are you going to do?" Gabe asked.

It was an excellent question and one that I couldn't answer.

"Dausseeeeee," Sister Catherine sang as she mooned me. "Yooouah aaaaandah meeeeeeeee!"

She flipped through the air and landed in a ghostly lump at my feet. Glancing down at her, I smiled and cupped her cheek. "Pull your pants up," I told her. "It's rude to show your ass while people are eating."

She laughed and did as I asked. "Nowww," she insisted, extending her arms to me.

My wing-woman wanted to talk. I glanced over at Gideon. He didn't look happy, but he nodded his head.

"Business as usual," he said, crossing the room and wrapping his strong arms around me. "Go with your gut. I believe in you."

"Business as usual," I repeated, holding him tight. "For us and for Mini-Daisy Gideonia."

The Grim Reaper laughed. The sound of his joy filled my empty tank in a way that nothing else could. The man was my reason, but I was my own strength. I was fine on my own two feet. However, his love made my world a much more beautiful place.

"I seriously hope she doesn't go with that name," Gabe muttered. "It's awful."

I ignored him. I knew exactly what I wanted to name our little girl, but that was a conversation I wanted to have alone with Gideon.

"Sister Catherine," I said. "Let's chat."

"Yaussssss, Dausseeeeee," she replied with a serene smile on her lovely decaying face. "Chaaaaaatah."

"Hug me," I told her. "I'll keep you safe."

"Aaaaandah Sissssstah Caaatheerinee keeeeep yoooouah saaaaaaafeeee toooah! Leeeetah usssssssss praaaaayeeeah."

I didn't want to tell her that I had no clue how to pray. I realized that wasn't exactly fitting for the Angel of Mercy. Maybe I could learn a thing or two from my butt-baring buddy.

∽

The cold. The cold went all the way to my bones and tore through my body like sharp, frozen daggers made of ice. Trying to catch my breath, I gasped for air and willed myself to stay calm.

I didn't fight the sensations. I welcomed them. I knew what was on the other side of the pain.

My head pounded violently and every single cell in my body screamed for oxygen.

And then it stopped. My body felt like it was floating on air. A slightly cool breeze ruffled my curls and I smiled.

"Sister Catherine," I called out as my breathing normalized. "Are you here?"

"Open your eyes, Daisy!" she said with a peal of laughter that made me smile wider.

The woman was a nut... and she was mooning me. No longer was her bare bottom ghostly. It was pink and plump. Since there were no floors or walls to speak of, she appeared to be floating midair with her rear end exposed.

"Seriously?" I asked, wincing. "You're mooning me?"

"Absolutely," Sister Catherine said, pulling up her pants with an ear-splitting grin. "Have to lighten the mood before it gets heavy."

"Did it work?" I asked.

"You tell me," she said, walking towards me with a naughty smirk.

"Umm... yes," I admitted. "Although, it seems kind of un-nunly to drop trou and show your bare bottom."

"You don't know many nuns, do you?" she asked.

"None," I said then giggled. "None nuns."

"We're a lively bunch," she informed me with a wink.

Sister Catherine was lovely. Her smile lit her hazel eyes and she exuded warmth. Her light brown hair was short and stylish. She was the same height as me, but had a few extra pounds on her frame. She was incredibly huggable and beau-

tiful inside and out. Just being near her felt magically calming.

"So how can I help you?" I asked.

She looked surprised. "I don't know what you mean."

Now I was surprised. "Well, you're here for a reason. You must have unfinished business. I can help you solve it so that you can move on."

The nun was stymied. She tapped her pointer finger on her chin, her brow wrinkled in thought. "Hmmm, I might have a library book I forgot to turn in before I died, but I'm sure Sister Esther will return it for me."

"Mmkay," I said, not sure how to proceed. That wasn't the way it worked. I was the one who helped the dead. "If you don't mind me asking, how did you die?"

"Cancer," she said. "Ran in my family, but I got forty-seven wonderful years out of my life. No regrets. Not a one."

"Well shit," I muttered, then slapped my hand over my mouth. "Sorry about that."

"You think nuns don't say an occasional potty word?" she inquired with a twinkle in her eye.

"Not a clue," I told her, still racking my brain as to why we were here.

"We do," she confided in me. "And we like beer too!"

If I had the time, I'd talk with her for hours. I didn't have the luxury.

"Sister Catherine, why did you want to talk?"

"I wanted to pray with you."

"Pray?" I asked as my face fell.

"Yes, child," she said.

She wasn't much older than me, but the endearment felt nice.

"Not to be rude, Sister, but I don't think I have time to pray. I kind of have a lot going on right now. Are you sure you don't need anything from me?" I had to get to the bottom line and get out. While having a friendly chat was wonderful, it was counterproductive to figuring out how to complete my mission.

"Just a few minutes of your time, Daisy. I think you might be my unfinished business."

I didn't know how to answer her. So I didn't. Following her lead, I bowed my head. Realizing I didn't actually know any prayers, I stayed quiet and listened.

"Our Father, Who art in Heaven, hallowed be Thy name; Thy kingdom come, Thy will be done on Earth as it is in Heaven. Give us this day our daily bread and forgive us our trespasses, as we forgive those who trespassed against us; and lead us not into temptation, but deliver us from evil. Amen."

"Are we done?" I asked.

"I don't know. Are we?" she countered. "What stood out to you in the Lord's Prayer, Daisy?"

I ran through it in my head. The word "forgive" popped out. That wasn't surprising considering what was going on. "Repeat the part about forgiveness again, please."

Sister Catherine smiled. "And forgive us our trespasses, as we forgive those who trespassed against us."

"I did that," I said. "I don't know what more I can do. I barely have any more time and I have no clue how much will be left when we get back."

"Time is the key," she said. "Use it. Recreate it. It only takes but a moment to forgive."

Sister Catherine embraced me tightly. It was full of love. I leaned into her and hugged her back. The moving target stopped *moving. The answer hit me like a ton of bricks. It was indeed right in front of me. Zadkiel had given me hints and Sister Catherine had helped reveal them. It was now time to use them.*

"May God bless you and watch over you," Sister Catherine whispered as we fell right back into reality with only moments of time left.

CHAPTER FOURTEEN

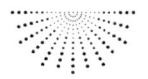

When I came to, everyone in the room was in a freaking tizzy. There were six new holes in the wall. I was sure they were compliments of Gideon. His thick blond hair stuck straight up on his head and he looked like he was about to lose his shit.

My mom and dad weren't faring much better. The Archangel paced the room like a tiger in a cage and my mother floated next to him, wringing her hands. Actually, no one looked good. Tim was curled up on the floor in a ball and Candy Vargo was literally eating her toothpicks. Gram didn't even chastise her. She just hovered near her to make sure she didn't choke.

Charlie had his arms wrapped around June and held her as she cried. Jennifer sat on the overstuffed armchair and drank wine straight from a bottle. So much for the no-booze rule. Missy and Heather sat pale and quiet on the love seat holding hands.

The Angels watched everyone with tense and guilty expressions on their faces. They thought they were to blame. They were and they weren't. I'd forgiven them for what they'd done. I hoped that if I still knew them in the future, they would never do anything like it again.

However, my future was in question. All of our futures were in question.

Maybe.

Only Sister Catherine was calm. She smiled at me and pointed to the hourglass. A lot of time had passed during our visit in her mind, and there was only a small bit of sand left. The *time* to move was now. I glanced at the draining hourglass. I was so close to having everything I wanted, and just as close to losing it all. My mind raced. Angel of Mercy. Forgiving trespasses. Forgiveness and judgement… I had judged someone, someone I hated with everything I was. I'd judged them without any forgiveness in my heart.

I groaned inwardly. The plan was insane. I was unsure if I could do it and truly mean it. It was so wrong on so many levels, but it was also right.

I looked around, sick to my stomach, at my family as they stared back at me with anticipation. "I know what I have to do." My entire body clenched. I took in the faces of the people I loved, possibly for the last time. "Send me back in time," I said to the Angels. "Now."

"To when?" Abby asked, standing up and raising her arms above her head.

"To the battle with Clarissa," I told her as I heard Gideon swear and punch another hole in the wall.

"Are you sure?" Gabe asked, jumping to his feet and raising his arms.

"Positive," I insisted. "Quickly please."

"It won't necessarily end the same," Candy Vargo warned.

"What do you mean?" I asked as my stomach plummeted. I hadn't even considered that as an option.

"If you're going to change what happened, Clarissa has the ability to change it as well," she cautioned.

"Don't go," Gideon said with such raw pain in his voice I felt it stab at my heart. "You could die. If Zadkiel sends you back, you'll live. It will be different, but you'll be alive. I can go on if I know that."

I shook my head and glanced at the hourglass. The top globe was precariously close to being empty. "Not worth it anymore," I said, needing him to understand and support me. "I won't have you. I won't have our baby. I won't have any of this. I'm meant to be the Angel of Mercy. I feel it in my gut. Please… trust my gut. Love me enough to trust me." I put my arms around him and gazed up at him. "Love me as much as I love you."

He was speechless for a moment. "I love you more than words can explain," he whispered brokenly. "I want you to live. You can still live a full life."

"It's not full without you in it."

He paused and searched my eyes for doubt. There was none.

"As you wish," he said softly. He kissed me so tenderly I thought I would break. "I will love you till the end of time, Counselor."

"Back at you, Reaper," I said, showing a brave face. If this didn't work, he might not remember loving me, but I couldn't allow myself to think about failure. "I'll be right back."

"From your mouth to God's ears," Prue said as she and Rafe stood up and raised their hands high.

"We will bring you back as well," Gabe told me.

I was glad someone thought I was coming back. "You sure about that?"

"Without a doubt," Abby promised.

"Godspeed, Daisy," Rafe said as all four slashed their arms through the air in unison.

I fell backwards in time.

And the situation in front of me was just as awful as the first time I'd experienced it.

∽

I WAS IN MY LIVING ROOM. THE SAME PLACE I WAS ONLY seconds ago, but in a very different time. Impossibly, I was the Daisy from two days ago, now. In her clothes. In her time. Pre-Clarissa showdown—but with full knowledge of the future. As always, the impossible was possible. I was proof.

"Thank you," I whispered as I closed my eyes and prepared for what I knew was about to come. I wasn't sure who I was thanking. Maybe the Angels. Maybe the Universe. Maybe God.

Did it matter? I wasn't sure and didn't have the time to figure it out.

I checked my body. It was fine, but a little stiff. Thankfully, I fell back through time and had landed in one piece. It was a good start. Showing up minus a few limbs wouldn't have ended well... for anyone.

Time travel was nothing like diving into the minds of the dead. It wasn't what I'd call comfortable, but at least I could breathe. It was the second time I was going to go through this, but I had to treat it as if it was the first. Keeping Candy Vargo's warning in mind, I sucked in a huge breath and focused on the now. My future depended on it.

"Mini-Daisy Gideonia," I said softly, touching my stomach. "This is for you. Stay with Mommy. And no matter what happens, I love you with all my heart."

A crash of lightning cracked open the sky. I felt it straight to my toes. My father's roar of fury and my mother's screams pierced my soul. The sound of her fear was devastating the first time and worse the second. Just as I recalled... our plans had been shot straight to hell.

We didn't need to go to Clarissa. She had come to us.

I pushed Missy into Tim's arms. "Protect Missy, Jennifer, June and my dogs. Make sure Candy and Gideon are not in harm's way," I ordered. "Send Heather and Charlie down. I'm going out."

"Is that wise?" Tim yelled over his shoulder as he and Missy rushed up the stairs.

"Wise isn't part of the equation," I shouted as more lightning ripped through the sky. *Please let me survive this time like I did the last.* "People I love are out there."

My body moved with the knowledge that it had done this before. I felt like I was inside myself and floating above myself simultaneously. It was strange and I didn't like it, but I went with it willingly. There was no other choice.

Running out the front door with speed I knew would render me invisible, I grabbed my mother and threw her as far as I could. If she'd been alive, she would have been broken in half. She was not. She was a ghost. If something fell off, I could glue it back on. If she was turned to ash and destroyed, there would be no way of fixing her.

"Daisy, GO," my father shouted above the wind. "This is my fight."

Clarissa's hands rose above her head. She slashed them in a downward motion and shrieked like a banshee. Seeing her again made my stomach roil. She was supposed to be dead. She wasn't, and neither was I at this point. Win-win. I was about twenty feet away and the barrier was forming fast.

"Dad, you're wrong," I whispered as I sprinted toward the barrier and prayed I would make it inside before it closed. I'd made it once. I could do it again. "This is *our* fight."

The magical wall enclosed the front yard only—the house and the surrounding woods were on the outside. In her deranged fury, Clarissa had been sloppy. I ran as if my life depended on it. I was aware her goal was my mother. She'd failed. I'd made sure of it then and I made sure of it now. She'd killed my mother once. Clarissa would not have the opportunity to do it again.

"Shit," I muttered. I knew I was about to break my toes, but went for it anyway. No pain, no gain.

I tripped over a large branch. The barrier slammed

down on my toes as it hit the ground, but I'd made it in. I grunted in agony as I grabbed my leg and yanked my foot through. It hurt as much the second time as it had only days ago.

"Ohhh," Clarissa purred, eyeing my father with naked lust. "What a lovely surprise. It's been a while, Michael."

She called my father by his celestial name. His hiss of disgust didn't bother her. Rolling behind a downed tree, I hid and waited for the opening I knew would come shortly. June's soul wasn't in her hands. It was in her pocket.

Movement in my periphery pulled my eyes from the prize for the briefest of moments. Heather and Charlie prowled the edges of the barrier like crazed animals, looking for a way in. There was no way in and no way out. I knew that as a fact. They did not.

Charlie's badassery was on full display. His entire body sparked with silver flame and his eyes were blinding beams of shimmering light. Heather's tattoos raced and danced along her skin at a dizzying speed. My friends looked like otherworldly predators, and I was determined to see them again.

Donna and Karen raced around the perimeter, growling and barking. My Hell Hound's eyes were as red as a Demon's. Her canines had extended and she gnashed them menacingly. Karen picked up on her sister's distress and snarled as she followed suit. My stomach tightened in fear for my dogs. The Angel of Mercy wouldn't think twice about destroying anything I loved. My dogs had lived through it before, my gut told me they'd make it again.

"Please be right, gut," I whispered, dreading what was coming.

"The game is over, Clarissa," my father said evenly. "You are done. Your crimes are reprehensible—unforgivable."

Clarissa adjusted the neckline of her torn and filthy dress to show more cleavage. Her eyes were a dull gold and dilated. The physical beauty that she'd once possessed was gone, replaced by the hardened shell of a woman who had lost her sanity. Her play for my father's affections was pathetic and sickening. But this time—unlike before—they tore at my heart.

Zadkiel's words raced in my mind. *"I left before I became desensitized. It's a dangerous proposition to lose your humanity. It serves no one. I was smart enough to end my journey before my journey ended me."* Clarissa's humanity was gone. She'd stayed far too long at the fair. It was a lesson I would carry with me always.

"Michael, what say you we let bygones be bygones and move ahead… together? Let's be us again."

"There was never an us," he informed Clarissa coldly.

She shook her head in a staccato rhythm of confusion or denial at his words. Her hands clenched at her sides and she tried to giggle seductively. It sounded tinny and deranged. My father's eyes met mine for a brief moment as he gauged the size of the barrier. They widened ever so slightly when he saw me. The raw fear in them when he realized I was trapped inside with him made my breath catch painfully in my chest.

I wanted to tell him it would be okay. I wanted to tell him that we were going to live… that we'd already lived through it. But the truth was murky. Even though we'd survived the first time didn't mean we would again.

It was all up to me.

"There was an us," Clarissa insisted shrilly. "There *is* an us. If it hadn't been for the whore, you would be mine. I did all of this for me… and you, of course."

My father eyed Clarissa with barely concealed hatred. His body language relaxed when he spotted my mother on the outside of the barrier. He tilted his head slightly to the left, signaling for my mother to hide. She nodded sadly, extended her arms to him and faded back into the trees.

"You see, it could be so simple," Clarissa continued, oblivious to everything going on around her. She ran her hands up and down her body in a repulsive attempt at seduction. "All we have to do is get rid of the evil ones. It hurts my feelings to be reminded of your silly indiscretion."

"Do you have June's soul?" he asked, tamping back his ire and keeping his tone conversational.

Clarissa took his lack of hostility as a sign of success. Her smile was lewd and she patted her pocket. "I do. I can give it back to you for a small price. Destroy Alana's soul for me. Show me your devotion, Michael."

"Alana has moved on," Clarence lied smoothly.

Clarissa glanced around wildly. "She was here. I saw her," she said, growing more agitated by the second.

"You must have seen another ghost. There are many in residence. Alana has left this realm."

Clarissa howled like a dying animal and shot a bolt of lightning at my father. He dodged it with ease just as he had the first time we'd played this lethal game. My breath came out in a whoosh of relief.

Everything I wasn't directly involved in seemed to be playing out exactly as it had before. The need to stand beside my dad made my heart race erratically and my muscles tighten to the point of pain. It was too soon. If I moved now, I could rewrite history in a deadly way. My body told me to move. My head insisted I wait.

I waited—just like I had before.

"I would have known if she'd moved on," Clarissa snarled, punching at the air around her. With each jarring movement she made, fires ignited and bolts of lightning struck the ground inside the barrier.

"Would you?" my father asked, staying calm. "You haven't exactly been in touch, so to speak, lately."

His words made the crazed Angel pause. Her face pinched in confusion as she debated the truth of what she'd just been told.

"Are you lying to me?" she demanded, rocking back and forth on her bare feet.

"Come now, Clarissa," my father said consolingly. "Would I lie to you?"

Clarissa walked in a tight circle, flapping her arms. With each step she took, she seemed to lose more of her tenuous grip on reality. I closed my eyes and tried not to cry. She was so incredibly broken it was gut-wrenching to watch. It didn't negate her vicious crimes or the truth that she destroyed everything she touched, but I could try to hate the sins and not the sinner.

Internally I warred with myself. Was I lying to myself

that I could forgive her? I couldn't love her. I didn't have it in me. Since I knew what was about to happen, I felt my hatred rise. How in the hell could I forgive—truly forgive—someone who I despised?

"No, of course not. You wouldn't lie to me, Michael," she said with a laugh of joy. "Everything I did, I did for us. You know that. You must know that." The pitch of her voice changed. It grew high and thin. "That woman was a *human*. You are an Archangel. It was blasphemy. I couldn't let that happen. She had to die."

"So, you chose to make decisions that were not yours to make?" he asked.

"Exactly," she shouted. "No one is real. We're all simply pieces of a machine. It's all a test. God is testing us." She glanced down at her hands and shook them like they were covered in spiders. "They think I'm crazy, but if they don't catch me, they can't prove it. And they will *never* catch me."

"Of course not," my father said, slowly moving closer to Clarissa.

"Did I tell you about the time I was chased by Demons in the woods?"

"No," my father said, glancing over at me, then pointedly at Clarissa's pocket where June's soul was hidden. "Tell me."

I nodded and shimmied on my stomach down the length of the tree to position myself closer.

This time, I knew that Clarissa was already aware of me even though she hadn't let on yet. Hindsight was twenty-twenty. It was also terrifying. Carefully, I matched every move that I'd made exactly. The room for error was slim and deadly.

"Demons," Clarissa hissed. "They began their attack in my dreams, then chased me through the woods. They steal your hair and peel your skin. They rape and leave their seed in the powerful ones like me. Did you know that?"

"I did not," Clarence answered, humoring her. "Must have been terrible. How did you escape?"

She paused as if she had forgotten what she was talking about. Pulling June's soul from her pocket, she rolled it like a ball in her hands. "I'm not sure I did escape," she said, then shrugged. "Will you kill my Demons? I killed for you. I think it's only fair you return my gift."

"Give me June's soul and then we can talk about killing Demons," he suggested, moving even closer.

"How about this," Clarissa countered with an excited squeal, skipping away from my father. She tossed June's soul into the air and caught it right before it hit the ground. "Since the whore you impregnated is gone, I want you to end the bastard who was produced to prove your love to me."

"I don't know where she is," my father lied again, making an attempt to stay in the vicinity of Clarissa's manic movement.

"I do," she screamed, aiming her free hand at the downed tree I was hidden behind, blowing it to bits. "Kill her or I will."

The debris from the explosion made seeing what was even inches in front of me difficult. However, I'd learned from Gideon that I didn't need my eyes to see. Closing them tightly, I dove through the dust and splintered wood in the direction of Clarissa's voice.

I knew the Angels weren't coming to save us, but the conversation had to match. I could do that. There was only one moment I needed to change and it hadn't arrived yet.

"Where are the Angels?" I shouted at my father as he tried to attack and restrain Clarissa. "They said they'd be here when the time was right. I think the time is right."

She moved like the wind and cackled with madness as she evaded my father.

"That's code for they'll be here when the battle is over," he yelled as he took a hit of magic from Clarissa that sent him hurtling into the side of the barrier.

My father's power wasn't fully back. He was in as much danger as June's soul. I just needed his involvement in the fight to stay the same. Getting to the end alive was the goal. Clarissa would still die. It had to happen. It was either her or us. However, our survival was still iffy according to Candy Vargo. Playing with the past was serious business.

"Oh my God," I choked out as it occurred to me that I could have asked the Angels to send me back to the final moments of the battle. They were literal and I hadn't been specific. I was an idiot. And very possibly a dead one.

Thankfully, my power was with me.

I was about to use it.

"Look at me," I shouted at Clarissa as she was poised to send another burst of magic my father's way. "You want me? Then come after me."

Her head whipped in my direction and the corners of her lips curled into a sneer.

"You will die like your mother—like a coward."

Even though I knew what was headed my way, it hurt

more than it did originally. The shot grazed my arm like a white-hot knife as I used my speed to avoid the brunt of it. Clarissa's eyes widened in surprise, and she followed up with another, more vicious streak of deadly enchantment.

Picturing a shield surrounding me, I sliced my arm through the air and prayed to every deity I could think of that it would work. If it worked once, it could work again.

The blast hit the invisible shield and bounced back, ripping through Clarissa with a furious hiss. She doubled over and roared with so much outrage, I slapped my hands over my ears. Time seemed to slow as I watched her shoot a bolt of blood-red lightning at my father. He took it head on. Staggering back to an upright position, he aimed his glowing hands at her feet.

"Grab the soul, Daisy," he bellowed as he threw a ball of fire at the bottom half of Clarissa.

Barreling through the heat of my father's magic was almost debilitating, but the object of my desire was so close. I knew I would fail. I had before and I would again. It didn't make me try any less hard than I had on the day it had actually happened. This part could *not* change.

Picturing June's smiling face and hearing her sweet giggle in my head, I pushed through the golden blaze that engulfed the lower half of the abomination who had destroyed so much that I loved.

"Mine," I snarled as I went to grab June's soul.

As before, I was fast.

And as before, Clarissa was faster.

With a psychotic laugh, she threw June's soul. It slammed against the side of the barrier and began to roll around the perimeter. "Good luck," she growled, shooting death blows at both me and my father.

Running at a speed that made me forget where I was for a second, I tried to catch June's soul. The faster it rolled, the faster I ran. Charlie's tortured bellow of anguish could be heard through the barrier.

"Come to me, please," I begged even though I knew I couldn't reach it. As before, I chased the orb that seemed to be spinning into oblivion.

Right as I was within reach, a disembodied hand shot up from the earth and disappeared with June's soul.

This time I knew who the hand belonged to, but I still fought to find the soul of my beloved friend. Crawling on the ground, I began to dig.

"If I can't have you, no one can!" Clarissa screamed in a fit of rage. "I'm just so terribly hurt you won't see your daughter die, Michael. But don't worry. I'll make sure it's far more painful than your demise."

Everything was a repeat. I'd already lived the ending. As long as the small rewrite didn't blow up in my face, I knew it would be over soon.

My body felt broken. My spirit was crushed. It was a horrid feeling.

Just a little longer, Daisy, I told myself. *Focus. Play to win.*

Turning my head, I gasped. My father was on the ground in a pool of his own blood as Clarissa continued to blast him with bolts of fire.

"Would you like a hug, Michael?" she inquired coldly as she moved in to wrap my father in a deadly embrace. "This will only hurt a bit, my love."

The picture was sickeningly familiar. She was about to squeeze the life from my father just as she had done to the ghosts, Anna and Mike. Clarissa was incapable of anything except death and destruction.

"Nothing is impossible," I said. "Nothing is impossible. Nothing is impossible as long as I believe."

I believed.

Raising my hands to the Heavens, I kept my eyes on Clarissa. "I believe," I whispered. "I believe that good outweighs evil. I believe that love can conquer hate. I believe *nothing* is impossible. I believe that forgiveness is divine. And I believe that I am the Angel of Mercy."

I'd felt true grace once in absolution. I would find that place again.

I covered the distance between us in less time than a blink of an eye. Faces raced through my mind as I wrapped my arms around Clarissa and pulled her away from my father. Gideon's face. My mother's face. Gram's face.

The images came faster—June, Missy, Heather, Jennifer, Tim, Candy, Sister Catherine. The faces were beautiful. The faces were love. Even the faces of Prue, Abby, Rafe and Gabe gave me hope and strength.

"Love trumps hate," I said as the feeling of fire lit with gasoline raced under my skin.

Clarissa's struggles didn't stop me, but they tore at my soul. Her vitriolic words didn't reach my ears. I heard Gideon's voice. My father's voice. My mother's voice. If these were my last moments, I was blessed to have the people I loved with me.

Staring at the murderous Angel in my arms, I kissed

the top of her head. Her struggles grew frenzied and desperate when she realized I was about to play her at her own game.

However, this time it would have a twist.

I squeezed. I squeezed as hard as I could. Red-hot rage consumed me. I was losing control. Had I come this far only to be the reason for my own failure?

My embrace was destroying her and my kiss was that of death. Zadkiel's words bounced in my mind. *"Remember that living forever is something that can destroy a mind. Have mercy on those who break."*

Clarissa was broken beyond repair. I was not, and I would not let this moment be the beginning of my downfall. I was better than that.

"Forgive us our trespasses as we forgive those who have trespassed against us," I shouted.

Clarissa was tragically damaged. She didn't deserve my forgiveness after what she had done. She'd killed my mother in cold blood. She'd been the physical catalyst in my husband's death and then tried to send him wrongly into the darkness. She'd kept me from my father for over thirty years. And she'd done her best to kill me.

"Judgment will be my savior or my downfall." I repeated Zadkiel's words and then recalled my own. "Always forgive, but never forget. If you do, you'll be a prisoner of your own hatred and doomed to repeat your transgressions for eternity."

Clarissa's eyes grew wide and her struggles stopped. She stared at me, but I wasn't sure she saw me.

"End me," she begged in a ragged voice that was filled

with so much pain it almost brought me to my knees. "I can't do this anymore."

I paused. Could I even do this?

"Do it," she snarled as her body convulsed in my arms. "If you don't, I will hunt you down and destroy everything you love."

It was impossible for her to change. She was beyond redemption and repair. I had no control over that nor was it my responsibility.

I only had control over my own actions. Hate the sin, not the sinner.

"I forgive you," I whispered in her ear. "It will be easier now. I promise. No more pain." I took a deep breath and gently kissed her forehead again. She didn't move a muscle. A serene smile pulled at her lips and for a brief moment I saw the beautiful woman that she once was. That woman had disappeared long ago, but if God was merciful, maybe she'd be given a chance to find her again. That was not my call.

"Please," she said quietly. "Now. I'm ready."

I cast the same spell that had come from her own lips. As I began to speak the words, my heart shattered for the broken Angel in my arms. I knew I was doing what was right and had to happen, but that made it no easier. "Into nothingness. Nevermore to be seen. Neither here nor there nor in between. Be gone, Clarissa. Your time is over. Godspeed."

She popped—then turned to ash in my arms. Her remains scattered as the barrier cracked and fell. My limbs felt like lead. The loud ringing in my ears made me dizzy.

Dropping to the ground, I let my head fall between my knees and I gasped for air.

And then I cried. I didn't cry the first time, but this was not the first time.

It was the very last.

I had again found true grace in forgiving the one who deserved it least—devastatingly sad and astoundingly beautiful.

The touch of my father's bloody hand on my cheek was the most wonderful feeling in the world.

"Is it over?" I asked as the sun rose higher in the sky.

"It is, Daisy," he replied. "Clarissa has been destroyed."

With an exhausted cry of anguish from the bottom of my soul, I fell forward in time.

CHAPTER FIFTEEN

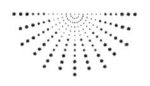

I was the same and I was different.

The fact was not up for debate.

From now until the day I took my last breath, I never wanted to visit the past again. The chances of destroying the future were too risky and could have devastating consequences.

It was a miracle that it had worked. The thought of tempting fate again made me shudder.

"Home sweet home," I whispered.

The living room was identical to the living room from the recent past. The furniture was familiar. The faces that watched me with trepidation were ones I knew—faces I loved. I was forty years old, but I felt like I'd lived a million years in a short span of time. The bone-weary exhaustion was real. Keeping my eyes open was a challenge.

The strong arms that scooped me up and cradled me were my home—safe and filled with love. But now, more than ever before, I knew I would survive even without the safe embrace of the man who I loved to a distraction. I would never want to, but I knew I could.

"Ding dong, the bitch is dead," Candy Vargo said, breaking the silence.

"Affirmative," I said. "Let me stand on my own," I told Gideon as he carefully put me down.

My knees were a little shaky and sleeping for a few days sounded like a fine plan, but my gut told me I wasn't quite done yet. I glanced over at my dad. He looked the same as he had before I fell back through time. But was he?

"Do you have more than one memory of what happened?" I asked. I did, but I was curious how much I'd changed the past.

He shook his head. "No. I don't."

"Does anyone?" I glanced around the room.

No one said a word. The Angels dropped to their knees and pressed their foreheads to the floor. That crap was going to have to stop. It made me wildly uncomfortable. Blind worship was a bad way to go. I didn't have the energy to get into it with them, but we'd get there.

Candy Vargo pulled out a toothpick and offered it to me. I stared at it for a long moment then took it and put it in my mouth. Gram raised a brow, but didn't say a word. I winked at her. She just shook her head and grinned.

"Nobody can recall the past in a way that it didn't happen," Candy Vargo said, handing out toothpicks to everyone. "I can, but I'm a freak of nature."

"Total freak," Tim said with a friendly nod of approval. Candy gave him a thumbs up.

"But I remember," I said, bemused that everyone in the entire room had toothpicks hanging out of their mouths. "I remember the way it went down the first and the second time."

Candy shrugged. "That makes you a freak too. Welcome to the club. It fuckin' sucks."

"Mmkay," I said with a wince. "Thanks… I think."

"Does this mean it's truly over? Daisy is safe?" my mom asked, still tense as she hovered in the air near my dad.

"Considering this has never happened before, I don't think it's a question we can answer," Charlie said.

June still looked twenty-five. Charlie had matched her age. It was startling to see them so young but knowing they were much older. And in Charlie's case… *much older*.

"It's over," I said. "Now it needs to be finished."

"Isn't that the same thing?" Tim asked, confused.

I laughed. The sound was forced. "You would think so."

"What's left?" Heather asked.

"I'm not sure," I told her honestly, walking over to the coffee table and examining the hourglass. Four single grains of golden sand were suspended midair in the bottom part of the globe. They hadn't joined the rest of the sand. Time had frozen for the shimmering granules.

Picking up the object that would determine my fate, I shook it. I needed the sand to fall. The journey wasn't over until all the miniscule pieces had united. No matter how hard I worked to make the sand move, it stayed exactly where it was suspended.

"Freaking awesome," I muttered, putting the celestial

time bomb down and backing away from it. "Jennifer, tell me a gross fact."

"Umm... now?" she asked, confused.

"Now. I need normal."

"That's considered normal?" Gabe asked with his nose on the floor.

"Yep. Get used to it," I told him.

Heather grinned. "I have one."

I raised a brow and grinned back at her. "Et tu, Brutè?"

"But of course," she replied, removing the toothpick from her mouth. "Our dear Jennifer has rubbed off on me like a fungus—a little smelly but not deadly."

"I'm not sure if that was a compliment or an insult," Jennifer said with a chuckle.

"Compliment," Missy promised, giving Heather a light elbow to her stomach. "Slightly shrouded but a compliment all the way."

"Go for it," I told my sister.

Heather rubbed her hands together and took a deep breath. I was glad she'd removed the toothpick. She would have inhaled it. I was too dang worn out to Heimlich anyone today.

"The inventor of Pringles chips was buried in a Pringles can," Heather shared triumphantly.

"How in the hell do you shove a body into a Pringles can?" Gram asked, scratching her head. "Must have been a monster-sized can."

"He was cremated," Heather explained with an expression that made it clear she regretted her choice to join the club.

"Ewww," June said. "There goes my love of Pringles."

"Not bad. Not bad at all," Jennifer congratulated Heather. "I give that an eight for weird. Only a three for gross."

"I concur," Tim said, pulling out his notepad. "Would it help if I gave you an example of historically interesting but factually disgusting?"

"Absolutely not," Heather said quickly.

"Very well then," Tim said, ignoring her. "Mary Shelley, the author of *Frankenstein*, kept her dead husband's heart in her desk drawer. It was there for a few years and finally discovered after she passed."

Gideon scrubbed his hand over his mouth and expelled a hissed stream of air through his teeth. I could tell he did *not* want to get involved, but he couldn't help himself.

God, I loved him.

"That makes no sense whatsoever," he said, giving up and diving into the gross fact fray.

"Wrong," Candy Vargo shot back. "Saw it. It was fuckin' gross. Hard as a rock."

"Correct! And I'm so jealous you got to observe it," Tim said. "Her husband was cremated, but his heart stayed intact. It was believed that it was calcified due to tuberculosis."

"I am so glad I'm not eating right now," Abby mumbled from her prone position. "These people are appalling."

I agreed and I loved it. "More," I said. "You're gonna have to up your game if you want to compete, Heather."

She rolled her eyes and shook her head. "Beware of what you wish for, Angel of Mercy."

"I can take it, Arbitrator," I challenged.

"So be it," Heather replied with a wicked glint in her eye. "There's poop in your coffee mug."

"Oh hell, I lied. I can't take it," I said with a groan.

"The Arbitrator is accurate," Tim assured me, much to my horrified regret of pushing Heather. "According to experts in environmental biology, twenty percent of coffee mugs contain fecal bacteria residue."

Jennifer cackled. "Remember that next time your coffee tastes like crap!"

"Are we done yet?" Candy asked with a gag. "I like my high-octane wakey juice. I can't take much more of this shit."

"We're done," I said, flopping down on the couch and pulling Gideon down with me. "So, so, so done." Closing my eyes, I sighed. If there was more to the game it would reveal itself when it was supposed to. Forcing it to occur could end in a shitshow.

"Daisy?" Jennifer said in an odd tone. "I don't wanna freak you out, but there's a floating golden ass hanging in your foyer."

My eyes shot open and I jumped to my feet. I was positive I'd heard her incorrectly—maybe she meant a floating golden donkey. Were there deadly donkeys? Right now, nothing would shock me.

It wasn't a donkey. Not even a little bit. It was definitely a floating golden ass. I knew exactly what was happening. It made me as happy as it made me sad. I was hoping for a little more time with my nutty friend.

Sister Catherine was no longer a decaying corpse of a

holy prankster. She appeared as she had when we'd met in her mind and she was bent over with her pants down. It was a moment I was pretty sure I wouldn't forget. It wasn't every day that a person was lucky enough to get mooned by a nun.

An ethereal and somewhat blinding golden glow surrounded my friend's bare butt as she cackled like a dummy. The mold had been broken when Sister Catherine was born and I was grateful for the brief time she was in my life. She was beautiful. Her smile and rear end would stay etched in my memories always.

Pulling up her pants and turning around, she giggled. "It's time, Daisy."

"I know," I said, walking toward her and extending my hand. The golden glow surrounding her was always so tempting to touch. It was warm and inviting—like silky liquid.

"Thank you," she said.

"I didn't help you," I reminded her, trying to memorize her face. "You helped me."

"Ahh, but you did," she said. "Doing for others is what always made me tick. You gave me one last opportunity to do what I was destined to do."

"Gonna miss you, Penguin," Candy said, flipping the nun off.

"Right back at you, jackass," Sister Catherine replied with a grin. "Remember your worth, Candy Vargo. You are a blessing. I see who you really are, my friend. Your light will illuminate the world if you let it. I will pray for you always."

"Probably gonna need that," Candy said. "Thank you, Catherine."

"And you, Daisy," Sister Catherine went on. "Stay true to who you are. You are very special indeed."

"You are too." I meant it with my whole heart. "Godspeed, Sister Catherine."

"How about a special send-off?" she suggested, glancing around the room with a naughty little smirk.

"Umm… what kind of special send-off?" I asked hesitantly.

"A group moon!" she announced to a roomful of laughter.

When the laughs finally died down, Sister Catherine put her hands on her hips and waited.

"Wait," my father said, alarmed. "Is she serious?"

"Dead serious," she replied. "Inappropriate nun-pun intended."

I shrugged and shook my head. "You people heard her. She wants a send-off moon. Drop your pants and give the nun what she wants."

"I can't believe I'm going to do this," Tim said, all atwitter. "I'm not sure anyone has ever seen my bottom."

"How is that possible?" Missy asked, unbuttoning her pants.

"Tim's a virgin," Candy announced.

Tim went purple in embarrassment. Waving his hand at Candy, he paid her back immediately. She was now ten years old again…. and pissed.

"Nope. No can do," Gram yelled as Candy went for Tim. "You deserved that, girlie. Tim's pecker business is not for public knowledge. That was rude and unacceptable. The boy just hasn't met the right person yet."

"He's a gazillion fuckin' years old," ten-year-old Candy grunted.

Just like before, it was alarming to see a child drop an f-bomb, but Candy Vargo was going to be Candy Vargo no matter the age.

"Don't matter," Gram told her, wagging her finger in her face. "That's Tim's business."

"Thank you, Gram," Tim said, still very pink.

"Not to worry," Gram assured him. "We'll get you signed up on one of them dating apps and find you a nice partner. Maybe someone who's into stamp collectin' since you're a mailman. Sound good?"

Tim was speechless. Gram didn't notice. She zipped out of the room and went to research dating apps for Tim.

"Excuse me," Gabe called out from his prone position. "Are we to show our asses as well?"

"Shut your mouth," Prue hissed. "You can never leave well enough alone."

"Yep," I said quickly before they started slapping and hitting each other… or worse. "It's a group effort."

"So silly," June said with a giggle. "I've never mooned anyone before."

"Get in a straight line," Gideon said with a barely disguised grimace and the tiniest of grins. "I have no desire to see any ass in here but Daisy's. If we line up, we can pay tribute—so to speak—to Sister Catherine without needing therapy from the viewing of mass ass."

"Fine plan," Charlie said, relieved. "This is a rather unusual request."

"I'm a rather unusual gal," Sister Catherine told him. "On three. One. Two. Three!"

Sister Catherine's peal of laughter was music to my ears. As quickly as we all dropped trou, we yanked our pants back up even quicker. It was a story I was sure would be told for a very long time.

I turned back to my friend as she began to fade away. Sister Catherine had been a piece of the puzzle that I would have been lost without. I watched her until she disappeared.

A thought occurred to me. It made me catch my breath and it made me smile. I wished I'd thought of it while she was still here, but I had a feeling she'd know.

"I want to call our daughter Alana Catherine—after my mom and Sister Catherine," I told Gideon.

Gideon's smile lit his eyes and I felt tingly all over. *"Perfect."*

It was. Our baby would be named for the woman who gave me life and the woman who gave me the ability to keep my life.

"Want to moon me later?" he asked with a wink.

"It's a date," I replied.

"Okay," Heather said, still grinning about the group moon. "Are we done *now*?"

"I vote for a yes on that," I said, pushing Gideon down on the couch and cuddling up next to him. "We're done for today."

"Are we?" Zadkiel inquired as he appeared in a silver flash of light.

The Angels dropped back to their knees in fear. That pissed me off. Everything about the combat-clad Angel pissed me off.

"I guess not," I said, staring daggers at the man who seemed determined to see me fail.

CHAPTER SIXTEEN

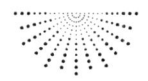

Zadkiel had forgotten his throne, but had brought along a few buddies to make up for it. They were faceless and terrifying. The air around them crackled with the promise of pain and agony. There were four of them wearing hooded purple robes that hid whatever horror was underneath. Gideon was on his feet so fast I didn't see him move. I followed quickly behind. The friendly atmosphere disappeared and in its place was a tension-filled standoff.

Zadkiel scanned the room. His eyes landed on the hourglass. "One more little test and you shall have earned your place."

"Who else do I have to forgive?" I demanded as I realized my hands were sparking. That was new. Thankfully, it didn't hurt. I was kind of done being beat up for the foreseeable future.

"Not forgive. Punish," he replied cryptically, seating

himself on my overstuffed chair like he was a welcome guest.

He was not.

"Unacceptable," Charlie hissed. "The parameters were set when the task was given. No changes can be made."

"Correct," my father ground out as he approached Zadkiel with a look in his eyes that made me want to hide.

Zadkiel shrugged. "Fine. Take them." He nodded to the faceless robed figures then pointed to the Angels on the floor.

I was unsure if the strangers had feet. They glided across the room like they were ice skating. It was unnerving and strange. As they approached the Angels, a fury larger than I knew I possessed lit up inside me. Images of the violent beginnings of my sisters and brothers flashed in my head. I'd never seen the faces of the beings who had meted out the punishments, but I was pretty sure that the four in my home were somehow involved.

"NO," I shouted as the abominations reached down to take the Angels. "Do *not* touch them."

Zadkiel smiled. It was ugly. "You said you weren't up for the mission. They are. I see no issue here."

"I see an *issue*," I ground out, crossing the room and standing between the Angels and their tormentors. "They're mine. My responsibility."

Zadkiel raised a brow. "You own them?"

Shoving my hands into the shallow pockets of my yoga pants, I willed myself not to blast the asshole. That was a move that was sure to end badly. Short-term wins could be long-term disasters.

"I don't own them. No one does. Not you and not *those things*," I said, nodding to the robed intruders. "Do you have any idea what was done to them? The criminal abuse?"

"Do you?" Zadkiel asked coldly.

I glared at him. I refused to drop my gaze. After what felt like an eternity, he was the first to lower his eyes.

"I do," I said, trying to keep the emotion out of my voice and failing. "I saw it. They were damned to absorb the sins of humanity. Who in the hell thought that was a good plan? It was despicable and inhuman."

"We are not human," Zadkiel pointed out. "The shades of gray are around every corner. Nothing is black and white. Do not judge what you can't understand."

He was right and all kinds of wrong. Maybe it wasn't my place to judge what had been done to my siblings, but I knew compassion from cruelty. The Angel might have thought he'd ended the journey before the journey had ended him, but he was incorrect. There was very little to no humanity left in Zadkiel.

A choice was in front of me. I was certain it was going to suck. However, there was no way in hell the Angels were leaving with the robed abusers.

"I will punish them," I said.

I heard Abby gasp. Prue began to cry. I wasn't sure if it was because they were happy I wasn't going to let Zadkiel have them or because they were upset I'd agreed to punish them.

"Do go on," Zadkiel said. "Let me hear how you will punish the ones who sinned against the Heavens. If it is acceptable, the grains of sand will join the others. As you might have noticed, there are four granules left. One for each of your *brothers and sisters*."

He made the words sound like curses. I wanted to make him eat them and choke.

The son of a bitch had put me on the spot. Physical harm was out of the question. They had been through that and it had warped them to the tipping point of no return. While forgiveness was divine, retribution seemed to be the way of the Immortals. If I was going to win this round, I had to lay out an acceptable plan.

"Help me," I said to Gideon frantically. "*I don't know what to do.*"

"*What is it that you want the Angels to accomplish?*" he asked.

"*I want them to find their humanity.*"

"*I believe the answer may lie in the word human,*" he replied.

My gaze shot to Gideon. A small smile pulled at his lips followed by a loud sigh. I was pretty sure he had hoped the Angels would leave. That might not be the case.

"The punishment will be for a set period of time. Pravuil, Abathar, Raphael and Gabriel will become human—no powers, no magic. When they have discovered—truly discovered—their humanity, their Immortality will return."

Prue continued to cry. Abby swore vitriolically under her breath. Rafe growled and I was pretty sure I heard Gabe chuckle. I was tempted to drop a barrier around them. I didn't need the celestial peanut gallery screwing up my plan to keep them from harm. Plus, the plan was good. If they were truly to serve humanity in a loving way, they needed to understand what it meant to be human.

"Rather mild," Zadkiel said, getting bored.

"Hardly. An Immortal without power is not *mild*," I countered. "What is the job of an Angel?"

"Read the bible," he shot back.

"On my list. Answer my question."

He sat silently and refused.

"Guidance, protection, proclamation, ministering care," the Archangel Michael said, moving to stand next to me, his daughter—and in front of his other children, who were basically on trial for their lives.

My father might have said that the Angels were no children of his, but his actions spoke otherwise. For a scary badass, he could be a softie.

"Blah, blah, blah," Zadkiel said with a disgusted eye roll.

Without any excess movement, the Archangel Michael approached the Angel Zadkiel and wrapped his hands around his neck. Lifting the huge man into the air, he leaned in close as Zadkiel struggled to breathe. "I was not finished."

Zadkiel grimaced as my father tightened his grip. "My apologies," he choked out.

Dropping Zadkiel to the ground, he turned and eyed the robed figures. If they had come for Zadkiel's protection, they sucked. They hadn't moved a single muscle to aid the Angel.

"As I was saying before I was interrupted," my dad continued as if choking someone was normal. Hell, maybe in Angel-land it was. "Assurance of divine presence, comfort, enlightenment—these are some of the key duties of an Angel."

"Then I win," I said. "My siblings have never had the opportunity to truly be Angels. It was stolen from them. I want to give them a chance. Not all punishments have to be violent. Trust me," I said, glancing over at the irate group on the floor. "It will not be pleasant or easy."

Zadkiel shrugged indifferently. "Not my call to make."

"I'm sorry. What?" I hissed, furious that he might take them anyway.

"Check the hourglass," he said flatly. "If the sand has moved, then your punishment shall stand. If it hasn't…"

"It has," Charlie growled. "The four grains of sand have joined the others. The Angels shall be rendered powerless until the time they find their humanity."

"Time," Zadkiel said, standing up and joining his faceless posse. "Such an interesting concept. Isn't it? The indefinite and continued progress of existence in the past, present and future."

"Your point?" I asked, tired of the cryptic games.

"When one manipulates the hours, minutes and seconds, there is a price to pay."

"The price?" I asked through clenched teeth. I was unsure if he meant me or the Angels. They had sent me back, but I'd requested that they do it.

Zadkiel shrugged. "It will become evident shortly. As far as the timeframe on your discipline methods go, or lack thereof… when the new Death Counselor takes her first breath, the *experimental punishment* of the Angels shall end. If they have not accomplished the task, they will be sent back from whence they came… never to leave again."

That was eight and a half months, give or take a few

days. Could centuries of abuse be replaced by compassion for humanity in that short a time?

"Is that negotiable?" I asked.

"It is not," he replied.

"Fine," I said.

"Daisy," Candy interrupted.

I held up my hand. I didn't need her to insult Zadkiel's privates. "I've got this."

"But—" she tried again.

"No buts," I told her. "I accept the parameters."

"As you wish," Zadkiel said with a look in his shrewd eyes that made me uncomfortable. "They have one month… starting now."

"Umm… clearly you don't know much about babies," I said.

"Clearly *you* don't know much about the punishment for manipulating time," he replied. "Oh, and I forgot to tell you—you know… that pesky small print. If the Angels do not accomplish the task, the first breath the new Death Counselor takes will also be her last."

I screamed and wanted to destroy him. Looking down, my flat stomach was no longer flat. I was about eight months pregnant. The *price* for manipulating time was now *evident*. The only thing evident to me was that Zadkiel had to go… straight to Hell.

Gideon roared in agonized fury. His body burst into red flame and he threw a blast of magic that took out the entire side of my house. My father dove for Zadkiel with rage that knocked my house right off its foundation.

But none of it touched the Angel. The purple robed

bastards shielded his pathetic ass from the aggression, then they disappeared in a blinding flash of light.

The silence in the room was louder than an explosion. My mind raced and my thoughts were jumbled and chaotic. Life just kept getting more difficult. Midlife was supposed to be a crisis, but this was a full-blown catastrophe.

"Why is he doing this?" I ground out through clenched teeth. Fury consumed me. "I played his stupid game." I threw up my hands. "And I won. I forgave my worst enemy to become the Angel of Mercy, and still, that asshole is making me jump through more deadly hoops. I don't understand." I looked to Gideon and to my father for answers. "You've been around since Time was a toddler. Is this part of the application process? I thought I already had the fucking job."

"He's always been the worst kind of bastard," Candy said, spitting on the ground as if warding off a curse.

Gram didn't say a word about me dropping the f-bomb and just winced when Candy deposited saliva on my carpet. Everyone was getting a free pass right now.

My dad shook his head. "Zadkiel is a wily son of a bitch. I don't know what he's playing at right now, but as the original Angel of Mercy, it's within his rights to challenge you. I'm sorry, Daisy. I'll do what I can to help, but there might only be one way through this." He cast a pithy glance at his four rotten apples.

I clenched my fists and consciously fought back the urge to blow up the house I loved so much into a pile of toothpicks. "Fanfreakingtastic."

Gideon stepped behind me and put his arms around my waist, his hands resting on my basketball-sized belly. "I will beat the humanity into those four if that's what it takes. Whatever needs to be done to make sure our child is born happy and healthy." He kissed the top of my head.

"One month," I said in a daze. I stared at the Angels on the floor. "Get up."

Slowly they rose to their feet. Prue's face was tear-stained and her lips trembled. Abby's eyes were narrowed to slits. Rafe wouldn't even look at me. Only Gabe was open and accessible. He rocked back on his heels and clasped his hands in front of him patiently.

"They can babysit for me," Candy Vargo said. "I got six foster kids coming to live with me next week. If caring for rugrats doesn't knock some humanity into them, I'm not sure what will."

As much as I wanted to express my shock at the news, I didn't. Candy Vargo, for all her crazy, had a hell of a lot of love to give. The language was iffy and the toothpicks were gross, but the heart was pure.

"I'll give them jobs at the bookstore," Missy volunteered.

"I'll teach them to bake cookies," June said.

"I'll set up a P.O. Box for each of you so you can send letters and receive mail," Tim announced. "I will also teach you disgusting knowledge. It's a wonderful icebreaker at luncheons with the gals."

The Angels looked alarmed. I wasn't sure if it was because they had no clue what a P.O. Box was or they feared Tim's *knowledge*.

"I'll teach them plumbing," Jennifer offered as Heather made a face. Jennifer had destroyed the entire plumbing system in the building Heather had purchased to house her law firm. Jennifer had done it to save Heather a few bucks. It had cost Heather time and a whole lot of money to fix Jennifer's *fixes*.

To my sister's credit, she didn't say a single word. She would happily pay plumbing bills till the cows came home if that's what it took.

"I shall make sure that the proper authorities have been notified and will look into bringing charges against Zadkiel," Charlie said. "I don't care what Michael says about his rights as the first Angel of Mercy. The bastard has overstepped."

"Couldn't agree more," Gram said to Charlie as she zipped in circles around the Angels. "I'm gonna teach y'all some manners and how to make my famous chicken salad."

"And I will be your stepmother," my mother said, floating over to the shocked Angels. "Daisy is my daughter. You are her father's children. I love Michael with everything I am. What comes from him automatically has my love."

The Angels had no clue what to do with that. Not one made a sound.

"Can I get in on that?" Heather asked with a shy smile.

"Already think of you that way, child," my mom told her. "And it thrills me."

My father hadn't stopped staring at the Angels since they'd stood up. He slowly approached them and stopped about a foot away. "I shall take you under my wing and teach you the true meaning of being an Angel."

"And I will kill all of you with my bare hands if you fail," Gideon added.

"Umm… that really doesn't go with all the other stuff," I pointed out.

"True," Gideon agreed. "But that's all I've got."

"Roger that," I said, then glanced over at the shellshocked Angels. "Are you in?"

"Do we have a choice?" Abby spat.

"No," I said in an icy tone. "You don't. I do not expect you to thank me for saving you from the faceless horrors. If you fail, those abominations will become your destiny." I placed my hands on my rounded belly and felt my little peanut kick me. "Failure is not an option. Dad, can you remove their power?"

"I can," he replied. "And I shall."

Crystals rained down in every color of the rainbow, illuminating the room in a kaleidoscope of shimmering hues. The Angels jackknifed forward in agony as their magic was ripped away. I bit down on my lip, so I didn't cry out. If they could be silent, so could I.

We had one hell of a journey ahead of us. Moving forward was necessary so I didn't curl into a ball and lose myself in the mother of all panic attacks. I would win. The life of Alana Catherine was on the line.

"Be nice," a voice whispered in my head.

"Gideon?" I asked, confused.

"No silly goose. I'm not Gideon," it replied. *"Listen closely. One will comply, one will lie, one will stand by and sadly one might die. You must determine the outcome."*

"Alana Catherine, is that you?" I asked as tears began to roll down my cheeks.

"I prefer Mini-Daisy Gideonia," she replied with a giggle.

"We can speak to each other?" I was amazed, shocked, thrilled and terrified that I might lose her.

"Just this once," she said. "Remember what I said, sweet Mommy, and tell Gideon not to kill them. That's mean."

"You call your dad Gideon?" I asked.

"Do you think he'll mind?" she asked, sounding all kinds of naughty.

"No," I told her glancing at Gideon who was watching me with interest. *"I believe he will be fine with whatever you want to call him."*

"I'll see you soon," she said as her sweet little voice faded away.

I wanted to beg her to stay and talk. I wanted her to tell me how to make the Angels comply. But mostly, I wanted to hold her in my arms.

I would do whatever I had to do to make that happen.

"I will only say this once," I told the newly mortal, powerless Angels in a harsh and painfully raw voice that seemed to be coming out of someone else's mouth. "You *will* find your humanity, or I *will* find it for you. Trust me when I say it will be far more pleasant if you do it yourselves. The life of my child is on the line, and losing her is not on the table."

Gideon and our very chatty child had lit up my midlife crisis in a profound and beautiful way. If the Angels didn't get with the program immediately, I'd light up their asses.

The path wasn't clear. The outcome was iffy. That didn't work for me.

Let the crisis continue. May the best Angel win.

Zadkiel assumed it would be him.

I was about to prove him wrong.

The End... for now

MORE IN THE GOOD TO THE LAST DEATH SERIES

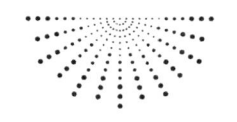

ORDER BOOK SIX NOW!

Midlife is madness—magical, messy and one freaking crisis after another.

With a new job I didn't apply for and an extended family I didn't know I had—midlife has become somewhat problematic. Gluing ghosts back together is easy compared to my new celestial occupation.

The Grim Reaper wants to put a ring on it. Tim wants to be a father. Candy Vargo has lost her damn mind and Jennifer thinks we're all sparkly vampires. I've been given an impossible task with catastrophic consequences for failure, but it wouldn't be my midlife without another crisis.

What's the saying? When in Crazytown, embrace the insanity or go insane. It's time to lean into the madness. I'm putting down roots, pulling up my big-girl panties and getting down to business. With one month to succeed, it's time to grow a bigger pair of lady-balls and play in the big league.

The rules are unclear. However, when it's a matter of midlife and death, I'm making the rules. And I will win.

EXCERPT: THE WRITE HOOK

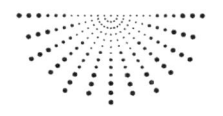

CHAPTER 1

"I didn't leave that bowl in the sink," I muttered to no one as I stared in confusion at the blue piece of pottery with milk residue in the bottom. "Wait. Did I?"

Slowly backing away, I ran my hands through my hair that hadn't seen a brush in days—possibly longer—and decided that I wasn't going to think too hard about it. Thinking led to introspective thought, which led to dealing with reality, and that was a no-no.

Reality wasn't my thing right now.

Maybe I'd walked in my sleep, eaten a bowl of cereal, then politely put the bowl in the sink. It was possible.

"That has to be it," I announced, walking out of the kitchen and avoiding all mirrors and any glass where I could catch a glimpse of myself.

It was time to get to work. Sadly, books didn't write themselves.

"I can do this. I have to do this." I sat down at my desk

CHAPTER 1

and made sure my posture didn't suck. I was fully aware it would suck in approximately five minutes, but I wanted to start out right. It would be a bad week to throw my back out. "Today, I'll write ten thousand words. They will be coherent. I will not mistakenly or on purpose make a list of the plethora of ways I would like to kill Darren. He's my past. Beheading him is illegal. I'm far better than that. On a more positive note, my imaginary muse will show his ponytailed, obnoxious ass up today, and I won't play Candy Jelly Crush until the words are on the page."

Two hours later…

Zero words. However, I'd done three loads of laundry—sweatpants, t-shirts and underwear—and played Candy Jelly Crush until I didn't have any more lives. As pathetic as I'd become, I hadn't sunk so low as to purchase new lives. That would mean I'd hit rock bottom. Of course, I was precariously close, evidenced by my cussing out of the Jelly Queen for ten minutes, but I didn't pay for lives. I considered it a win.

I'd planned on folding the laundry but decided to vacuum instead. I'd fold the loads by Friday. It was Tuesday. That was reasonable. If they were too wrinkled, I'd simply wash them again. No biggie. After the vacuuming was done, I rearranged my office for thirty minutes. I wasn't sure how to Feng Shui, but after looking it up on my phone, I gave it a half-assed effort.

Glancing around at my handiwork, I nodded. "Much better. If the surroundings are aligned correctly, the words will flow magically. I hope."

Two hours later…

CHAPTER 1

"Mother humper," I grunted as I pushed my monstrosity of a bed from one side of the bedroom to the other. "This weighs a damn ton."

I'd burned all the bedding seven weeks ago. The bonfire had been cathartic. I'd taken pictures as the five hundred thread count sheets had gone up in flame. I'd kept the comforter. I'd paid a fortune for it. It had been thoroughly saged and washed five times. Even though there was no trace of Darren left in the bedroom, I'd been sleeping in my office.

The house was huge, beautiful… and mine—a gorgeously restored Victorian where I'd spent tons of time as a child. It had an enchanted feel to it that I adored. I didn't need such an enormous abode, but I loved the location—the middle of nowhere. The internet was iffy, but I solved that by going into town to the local coffee shop if I had something important to download or send.

Darren, with the wandering pecker, thought he would get a piece of the house. He was wrong. I'd inherited it from my whackadoo grandmother and great-aunt Flip. My parents hadn't always been too keen on me spending so much time with Granny and Aunt Flip growing up, but I adored the two old gals so much they'd relented. Since I spent a lot of time in an imaginary dream world, my mom and dad were delighted when I related to actual people—even if they were left of center.

Granny and Flip made sure the house was in my name only—nontransferable and non-sellable. It was stipulated that I had to pass it to a family member or the Historical Society when I died. Basically, I had life rights. It was as if

CHAPTER 1

Granny and Aunt Flip had known I would waste two decades of my life married to a jackhole who couldn't keep his salami in his pants and would need someplace to live. God rest Granny's insane soul. Aunt Flip was still kicking, although I hadn't seen her in a few years.

Aunt Flip put the K in kooky. She'd bought a cottage in the hills about an hour away and grew medicinal marijuana —before it was legal. The old gal was the black sheep of the family and preferred her solitude and her pot to company. She hadn't liked Darren a bit. She and Granny both had worn black to my wedding. Everyone had been appalled— even me—but in the end, it made perfect sense. I had to hand it to the old broads. They'd been smarter than me by a long shot. And the house? It had always been my charmed haven in the storm.

Even though there were four spare bedrooms plus the master suite, I chose my office. It felt safe to me.

Thick Stella preferred my office, and I needed to be around something that had a heartbeat. It didn't matter that Thick Stella was bitchy and swiped at me with her deadly kitty claws every time I passed her. I loved her. The feeling didn't seem mutual, but she hadn't left me for a twenty-three-year-old with silicone breast implants and huge, bright white teeth.

"Thick Stella, do you think Sasha should wear red to her stepmother's funeral?" I asked as I plopped down on my newly Feng Shuied couch and narrowly missed getting gouged by my cat. "Yes or no? Hiss at me if it's a yes. Growl at me if it's a no."

Thick Stella had a go at her privates. She was useless.

CHAPTER 1

"That wasn't an answer." I grabbed my laptop from my desk. Deciding it was too dangerous to sit near my cat, I settled for the love seat. The irony of the piece of furniture I'd chosen didn't escape me.

"I think she should wear red," I told Thick Stella, who didn't give a crap what Sasha wore. "Her stepmother was an asshat, and it would show fabu disrespect."

Typing felt good. Getting lost in a story felt great. I dressed Sasha in a red Prada sheath, then had her behead her ex-husband with a dull butter knife when he and his bimbo showed up unexpectedly to pay their respects at the funeral home. It was a bloodbath. Putting Sasha in red was an excellent move. The blood matched her frock to a T.

Quickly rethinking the necessary murder, I moved the scene of the decapitation to the empty lobby of the funeral home. It would suck if I had to send Sasha to prison. She hadn't banged Damien yet, and everyone was eagerly awaiting the sexy buildup—including me. It was the fourth book in the series, and it was about time they got together. The sexual tension was palpable.

"What in the freaking hell?" I snapped my laptop shut and groaned. "Sasha doesn't have an ex-husband. I can't do this. I've got nothing." Where was my muse hiding? I needed the elusive imaginary idiot if I was going to get any writing done. "Chauncey, dammit, where are you?"

"My God, you're loud, Clementine," a busty, beautiful woman dressed in a deep purple Regency gown said with an eye roll.

She was seated on the couch next to Thick Stella, who barely acknowledged her. My cat attacked strangers and

CHAPTER 1

friends. Not today. My fat feline simply glanced over at the intruder and yawned. The cat was a traitor.

Forget the furry betrayer. How in the heck did the woman get into my house—not to mention my office—without me seeing her enter? For a brief moment, I wondered if she'd banged my husband too but pushed the sordid thought out of my head. She looked to be close to thirty—too old for the asshole.

"Who are you?" I demanded, holding my laptop over my head as a weapon.

If I threw it and it shattered, I would be screwed. I couldn't remember the last time I'd backed it up. If I lost the measly, somewhat disjointed fifty thousand words I'd written so far, I'd have to start over. That wouldn't fly with my agent or my publisher.

"Don't be daft," the woman replied. "It's rather unbecoming. May I ask a question?"

"No, you may not," I shot back, trying to place her.

She was clearly a nutjob. The woman was rolling up on thirty but had the vernacular of a seventy-year-old British society matron. She was dressed like she'd walked off the set of a film starring Emma Thompson. Her blonde hair shone to the point of absurdity and was twisted into an elaborate up-do. Wispy tendrils framed her perfectly heart-shaped face. Her sparkling eyes were lavender, enhanced by the over-the-top gown she wore.

Strangely, she was vaguely familiar. I just couldn't remember how I knew her.

"How long has it been since you attended to your hygiene?" she inquired.

CHAPTER 1

Putting my laptop down and picking up a lamp, I eyed her. I didn't care much for the lamp or her question. I had been thinking about Marie Condo-ing my life, and the lamp didn't bring me all that much joy. If it met its demise by use of self-defense, so be it. "I don't see how that's any of your business, lady. What I'd suggest is that you leave. Now. Or else I'll call the police. Breaking and entering is a crime."

She laughed. It sounded like freaking bells. Even though she was either a criminal or certifiable, she was incredibly charming.

"Oh dear," she said, placing her hand delicately on her still heaving, milky-white bosom. "You are so silly. The constable knows quite well that I'm here. He advised me to come."

"The constable?" I asked, wondering how far off her rocker she was.

She nodded coyly. "Most certainly. We're all terribly concerned."

I squinted at her. "About my hygiene?"

"That, amongst other things," she confirmed. "Darling girl, you are not an ace of spades or, heaven forbid, an adventuress. Unless you want to be an ape leader, I'd recommend bathing."

"Are you right in the head?" I asked, wondering where I'd left my damn cell phone. It was probably in the laundry room. I was going to be murdered by a nutjob, and I'd lost my chance to save myself because I'd been playing Candy Jelly Crush. The headline would be horrifying—*Homeless-looking, Hygiene-free Paranormal Romance Author Beheaded by Victorian Psycho.*

CHAPTER 1

If I lived through the next hour, I was deleting the game for good.

"I think it would do wonders for your spirit if you donned a nice tight corset and a clean chemise," she suggested, skillfully ignoring my question. "You must pull yourself together. Your behavior is dicked in the nob."

I sat down and studied her. My about-to-be-murdered radar relaxed a tiny bit, but I kept the lamp clutched tightly in my hand. My gut told me she wasn't going to strangle me. Of course, I could be mistaken, but Purple Gal didn't seem violent—just bizarre. Plus, the lamp was heavy. I could knock her ladylike ass out with one good swing.

How in the heck did I know her? College? Grad School? The grocery store? At forty-two, I'd met a lot of people in my life. Was she with the local community theater troop? I was eighty-six percent sure she wasn't here to off me. However, I'd been wrong about life-altering events before—like not knowing my husband was boffing someone young enough to have been our daughter.

"What language are you speaking?" I spotted a pair of scissors on my desk. If I needed them, it was a quick move to grab them. I'd never actually killed anyone except in fictitious situations, but there was a first time for everything.

Pulling an embroidered lavender hankey from her cleavage, she clutched it and twisted it in her slim fingers. "Clementine, *you* should know."

"I'm at a little disadvantage here," I said, fascinated by the batshit crazy woman who'd broken into my home. "You seem to know my name, but I don't know yours."

And that was when the tears started. Hers. Not mine.

CHAPTER 1

"Such claptrap. How very unkind of you, Clementine," she burst out through her stupidly attractive sobs.

It was ridiculous how good the woman looked while crying. I got all blotchy and red, but not the mystery gal in purple. She grew even more lovely. It wasn't fair. I still had no clue what the hell she was talking about, but on the off chance she might throw a tantrum if I asked more questions, I kept my mouth shut.

And yes, she had a point, but my *hygiene* was none of her damn business. I couldn't quite put my finger on the last time I'd showered. If I had to guess, it was probably in the last five to twelve days. I was on a deadline for a book. To be more precise, I was late for my deadline on a book. I didn't exactly have time for personal sanitation right now.

And speaking of deadlines...

"How about this?" My tone was excessively polite. I almost laughed. The woman had illegally entered my house, and I was behaving like she was a guest. "I'll take a shower later today after I get through a few pivotal chapters. Right now, you should leave so I can work."

"Yes, of course," she replied, absently stroking Fat Stella, who purred. If I'd done that, I would be minus a finger. "It would be dreadfully sad if you were under the hatches."

I nodded. "Right. That would, umm... suck."

The woman in purple smiled. It was radiant, and I would have sworn I heard birds happily chirping. I was losing it.

"Excellent," she said, pulling a small periwinkle velvet bag from her cleavage. I wondered what else she had stored in there and hoped there wasn't a weapon. "I shall leave you with two gold coins. While the Grape Nuts were tasty, I

CHAPTER 1

would prefer that you purchase some Lucky Charms. I understand they are magically delicious."

"It was you?" I asked, wildly relieved that I hadn't been sleep eating. I had enough problems at the moment. Gaining weight from midnight dates with cereal wasn't on the to-do list.

"It was," she confirmed, getting to her feet and dropping the coins into my hand. "The consistency was quite different from porridge, but I found it tasty—very crunchy."

"Right… well… thank you for putting the bowl in the sink." Wait. Why the hell was I thanking her? She'd wandered in and eaten my Grape Nuts.

"You are most welcome, Clementine," she said with a disarming smile that lit up her unusual eyes. "It was lovely finally meeting you even if your disheveled outward show is entirely astonishing."

I was reasonably sure I had just been insulted by the cereal lover, but it was presented with excellent manners. However, she did answer a question. We hadn't met. I wasn't sure why she seemed familiar. The fact that she knew my name was alarming.

"Are you a stalker?" I asked before I could stop myself.

I'd had a few over the years. Being a *New York Times* bestselling author was something I was proud of, but it had come with a little baggage here and there. Some people seemed to have difficulty discerning fiction from reality. If I had to guess, I'd say Purple Gal might be one of those people.

I'd only written one Regency novel, and that had been at the beginning of my career, before I'd found my groove in

CHAPTER 1

paranormal romance. I was way more comfortable writing about demons and vampires than people dressed in top hats and hoopskirts. Maybe the crazy woman had read my first book. It hadn't done well, and for good reason. It was over-the-top bad. I'd blocked the entire novel out of my mind. Live and learn. It had been my homage to Elizabeth Hoyt well over a decade ago. It had been clear to all that I should leave Regency romance to the masters.

"Don't be a Merry Andrew," the woman chided me. "Your bone box is addled. We must see to it at once. I shall pay a visit again soon."

The only part of her gibberish I understood was that she thought she was coming back. Note to self—change all the locks on the doors. Since it wasn't clear if she was packing heat in her cleavage, I just smiled and nodded.

"Alrighty then…" I was unsure if I should walk her to the door or if she would let herself out. Deciding it would be better to make sure she actually left instead of letting her hide in my pantry to finish off my cereal, I gestured to the door. "Follow me."

Thick Stella growled at me. I was so tempted to flip her off but thought it might earn another lecture from Purple Gal. It was more than enough to be lambasted for my appearance. I didn't need my manners picked apart by someone with a tenuous grip on reality.

My own grip was dubious as it was.

"You might want to reconsider breaking into homes," I said, holding the front door open. "It could end badly—for you."

Part of me couldn't believe that I was trying to help the

CHAPTER 1

nutty woman out, but I couldn't seem to stop myself. I kind of liked her.

"I'll keep that in mind," she replied as she sauntered out of my house into the warm spring afternoon. "Remember, Clementine, there is always sunshine after the rain."

As she made her way down the long sunlit, tree-lined drive, she didn't look back. It was disturbingly like watching the end of a period movie where the heroine left her old life behind and walked proudly toward her new and promising future.

Glancing around for a car, I didn't spot one. Had she left it parked on the road so she could make a clean getaway after she'd bludgeoned me? Had I just politely escorted a murderer out of my house?

Had I lost it for real?

Probably.

As she disappeared from sight, I felt the weight of the gold coins still clutched in my hand. Today couldn't get any stranger.

At least, I hoped not.

Opening my fist to examine the coins, I gasped. "What in the heck?"

There was nothing in my hand.

Had I dropped them? Getting down on all fours, I searched. Thick Stella joined me, kind of—more like watched me as I crawled around and wondered if anything that had just happened had actually happened.

"Purple Gal gave me coins to buy Lucky Charms," I told my cat, my search now growing frantic. "You saw her do it. Right? She sat next to you. And you didn't attack her. *Right?*"

CHAPTER 1

Thick Stella simply stared at me. What did I expect? If my cat answered me, I'd have to commit myself. That option might still be on the table. Had I just imagined the entire exchange with the strange woman? Should I call the cops?

"And tell them what?" I asked, standing back up and locking the front door securely. "That a woman in a purple gown broke in and ate my cereal while politely insulting my hygiene? Oh, and she left me two gold coins that disappeared in my hand as soon as she was out of sight? That's not going to work."

I'd call the police if she came back, since I wasn't sure she'd been here at all. She hadn't threatened to harm me. Purple Gal had been charming and well-mannered the entire time she'd badmouthed my cleanliness habits. And to be quite honest, real or not, she'd made a solid point. I could use a shower.

Maybe four months of wallowing in self-pity and only living inside the fictional worlds I created on paper had taken more of a toll than I was aware of. Getting lost in my stories was one of my favorite things to do. It had saved me more than once over the years. It was possible that I'd let it go too far. Hence, the Purple Gal hallucination.

Shit.

First things first. Delete Candy Jelly Crush. Getting rid of the white noise in my life was the first step to… well, the first step to something.

I'd figure it out later.

HIT HERE TO ORDER THE WRITE HOOK!!!!!

ROBYN'S BOOK LIST

(IN CORRECT READING ORDER)

<u>HOT DAMNED SERIES</u>
Fashionably Dead
Fashionably Dead Down Under
Hell on Heels
Fashionably Dead in Diapers
A Fashionably Dead Christmas
Fashionably Hotter Than Hell
Fashionably Dead and Wed
Fashionably Fanged
Fashionably Flawed
A Fashionably Dead Diary
Fashionably Forever After
Fashionably Fabulous
A Fashionable Fiasco
Fashionably Fooled
Fashionably Dead and Loving It
Fashionably Dead and Demonic

GOOD TO THE LAST DEATH SERIES
It's a Wonderful Midlife Crisis
Whose Midlife Crisis Is It Anyway?
A Most Excellent Midlife Crisis
My Midlife Crisis, My Rules
You Light Up My Midlife Crisis
It's A Matter of Midlife and Death

SHIFT HAPPENS SERIES
Ready to Were
Some Were in Time
No Were To Run
Were Me Out
Were We Belong

MAGIC AND MAYHEM SERIES
Switching Hour
Witch Glitch
A Witch in Time
Magically Delicious
A Tale of Two Witches
Three's A Charm
Switching Witches
You're Broom or Mine?
The Bad Boys of Assjacket

SEA SHENANIGANS SERIES
Tallulah's Temptation
Ariel's Antics
Misty's Mayhem

Petunia's Pandemonium
Jingle Me Balls

A WYLDE PARANORMAL SERIES
Beauty Loves the Beast

HANDCUFFS AND HAPPILY EVER AFTERS SERIES
How Hard Can it Be?
Size Matters
Cop a Feel

If after reading all the above you are still wanting more adventure and zany fun, read *Pirate Dave and His Randy Adventures*, the romance novel budding novelist Rena helped wicked Evangeline write in *How Hard Can It Be?*

Warning: Pirate Dave Contains Romance Satire, Spoofing, and Pirates with Two Pork Swords.

NOTE FROM THE AUTHOR

If you enjoyed reading *You Light Up My Midlife Crisis*, please consider leaving a positive review or rating on the site where you purchased it. Reader reviews help my books continue to be valued by resellers and help new readers make decisions about reading them.

You are the reason I write these stories and I sincerely appreciate each of you!

Many thanks for your support,
~ Robyn Peterman

Want to hear about my new releases?
Visit robynpeterman.com and join my mailing list!

ABOUT ROBYN PETERMAN

Robyn Peterman writes because the people inside her head won't leave her alone until she gives them life on paper. Her addictions include laughing really hard with friends, shoes (the expensive kind), Target, Coke (the drink not the drug LOL) with extra ice in a Yeti cup, bejeweled reading glasses, her kids, her super-hot hubby and collecting stray animals.

A former professional actress with Broadway, film and T.V. credits, she now lives in the South with her family and too many animals to count.

Writing gives her peace and makes her whole, plus having a job where she can work in sweatpants works really well for her.